If We're *Breathing, We're Serving*

If We're *Breathing,* We're *Serving*

Lifting the World, Book 1

FERRELL HORNSBY

Phase Publishing, LLC
Seattle

Phase Publishing, LLC first paperback edition
April 2020

ISBN 978-1-952103-07-0
Library of Congress Control Number: 2020905487
Cataloging-in-Publication Data on file.

Dedication

I dedicate this to my sweet husband, and to all who have helped him as he's learned how to live a vibrant and fulfilling life despite MS.

I also dedicate it to the amazing people everywhere who find ways to serve, no matter what their own circumstances may be. Thank you for your examples!

Prologue

December 21, 1994
Pine Valley, Idaho

"Hey, Frank, you've got a customer," his neighbor called from across the fence.

Frank Berglund looked up from the evergreen limbs he was stacking.

"Thanks, Pete," he called back.

He glanced around the small Christmas tree lot and spotted the young couple looking at a beautiful blue spruce near the front of the lot. That particular tree was nearly sixty dollars, he recalled.

As he wandered closer, he saw the haggard-looking husband glance at the price tag and shake his head. His wife's face fell, and Frank heard a couple of little voices expressing their own disappointment. Peeking around a tall, thin, fir tree, he saw two children; a girl who seemed to be about six years old, and a boy who was probably a couple of years younger. They were dressed for the weather. At least, they were both wearing coats and knitted hats. Looking back at the couple, he saw the woman's sweater was thin. It certainly wasn't going to keep much of the bitter cold wind from chilling her. The man's slightly thicker coat was worn at the elbows and frayed around the bottom.

Putting on his cheeriest smile, Frank approached the little family.

"Welcome to Berglund's Tree Lot," he greeted them. Reaching into his pocket, he pulled out two full-sized candy canes. Kneeling in front of the children, Frank cocked his head. "Could I interest you in a little Christmas candy?"

Hope in their eyes, they looked at their mother. She nodded, smiling.

They reached for the canes, but Frank held them just out of their grasp.

"Hm," he mused. "I think someone has forgotten the magic word."

"Please?" the little girl offered quickly.

Her little brother nodded wisely and added, "Pwease?"

"Absolutely!" Frank grinned and gave them each a candy cane.

Standing to face the couple, he noted the proud expressions they gave their children.

Good people, he thought, and smiled.

"I'm Frank Berglund. I haven't seen you here before, have I?"

The husband shook his head. "We just moved here from Kansas City. I'm Kevin Sawyer. This is my wife, Martha."

"It's nice to meet you. Welcome to Pine Valley. Now, what kind of tree were you thinking of?" he asked, already suspecting what they'd say.

"Something not too big," Kevin answered quietly.

"But I'd like a pretty shape. Do you have something like that?" Martha asked hopefully.

Frank stroked his chin thoughtfully. "Hm. How tall is your ceiling, and how large is the space you're thinking of putting it in?"

Kevin looked at his wife, whose expression was both hopeful and sad.

"Our ceilings are the standard eight feet high, and I think we can clear a three- or four-foot area in front of the living room window…" Kevin hesitated, then leaned forward and whispered, "but we can't afford a tree that big."

Frank nodded. "I understand. Tell you what, I think I have just the tree for you." He pointed to a little makeshift building in one corner of the lot. "Why don't you step into the Cocoa Shack and have a cookie and a cup of hot cocoa while I pull it out for you to look at? It's warmer in there out of the wind."

He got them settled inside, then trotted over to the six-foot trees. He picked out a beautiful blue spruce similar to the one they'd been eyeing. Carrying it to a back corner, he grabbed a hand axe and went to work. In a few moments, he stood back and grinned, then picked up the doctored tree and carried it to the Cocoa Shack. He leaned it against the wall and opened the door.

Children's laughter greeted him, and he grinned.

Cookies have that effect on children, he thought happily.

"Kevin, Martha, would you like to see what I've got?"

They joined him outside, and Martha gasped. "It's beautiful!" Then her face fell. "But I'm sure this is too expensive, Mr. Berglund."

"Please, call me Frank," he invited. "What you're seeing is the pretty side. I can't sell it for the same price that I'd put on a perfect tree, though."

He turned the tree around to show the back. "See here? There's a large gap in the base row of limbs. That flaw makes it hard to sell. It's completely uneven!"

Sneaking a peek at Martha's face, he knew he was on the right track. She was obviously daring to hope. "We could put the flawed side next to the wall. The sill is high enough that it won't show, right, Kevin?"

"But the other sides are perfect," Kevin argued. "Surely you couldn't knock off enough for us to…"

"Nonsense!" Frank interrupted. "At Berglund's Tree Lot, we only allow perfect trees to leave at full price. Nope. This one's got to be discounted."

"How much?" Martha asked tentatively.

"Tell you what. If you'll allow me to deliver this and get it set up for you, I can let you have it for…" He cocked his head, studying the tree from all sides. "I can't let it go for less than fifteen dollars."

"Fifteen…" Kevin choked. "I…"

Frank lifted his hands in surrender. "You're right. That's too much for such an imperfect tree. Ten dollars and that's my final offer." He looked around conspiratorially, then whispered, "I'll even throw in a few pine boughs for decorating purposes. What do you say?"

"I say that's not enough," Kevin argued. "I…"

Martha put her hand on her husband's arm. "It's Christmas, dear. Let's not deprive this good man of the blessings from a Christmas kindness."

Kevin opened his mouth, then closed it again, nodding. Turning to Frank, he stuck out his hand. "Deal."

Frank shook Kevin's hand warmly, then turned to Martha. "We close at nine. Would that be too late, or shall I bring it by tomorrow, instead?"

"Tonight will be fine," Martha answered gratefully. "We'll have the space cleared and ready."

As the couple gathered their children and made their way to the old station wagon parked in the road, Frank grinned to himself.

That was fun, he thought.

Later that night, after he'd delivered the tree and boughs, he said a silent prayer.

Thank you, God, he thought. *Thank you for the chance to brighten their Christmas.*

Chapter 1

January 1995

Frank raced to the bus stop, knowing he was late. The January thaw had made slushy puddles that he carefully avoided as he ran. He was almost there when he tried to jump a puddle, stumbled, and fell, nearly knocking over an older gentleman with a dog.

Rolling over and pushing himself up on his knees, Frank panted, "I'm sorry. I was so intent on catching the bus that I wasn't paying attention. Are you all right? Is your dog okay?"

"I'm fine," the man chuckled holding out a hand to help him up. "Bessie saw you and pushed me out of the way."

He looked down at the beautiful golden retriever and patted her head. "Good girl."

Their conversation was cut short when the bus arrived. Frank chose a seat near them and watched in fascination as the man settled his dog under the seat. That's when he noticed that the dog had on a vest, the kind blind people use with their seeing-eye dogs.

"Oh, I'm sorry," he stammered. "I didn't…"

Laughing, the man interrupted. "Oh, no. I'm not blind. I'm a guide dog puppy trainer. My name's Carl Peterson." He stuck his hand out with a smile.

Shaking his hand, Frank returned his smile. "I'm Frank Berglund. I have to say, I'm intrigued. I've never heard of such a thing."

"Most people haven't. Bessie is the fourteenth puppy I've trained," Carl said proudly.

"How do you train a puppy to be a guide dog?"

Shaking his head, the trainer smiled. "I don't actually do the guide dog part of the training. My task is to get her used to people and situations. She learns how to behave politely in public, where to walk, and where to lie down. I teach her to how to stay focused on her job and not become distracted, how to watch for danger, and to stay right with me no matter what. She certainly did her job today, eh, girl?" He patted her head again, and Bessie happily wagged her tail under the seat, creating a cheerful thumping sound.

"That's amazing!" Frank exclaimed. "Does it pay well?"

Carl's laugh was jolly. "I don't do it for the money. They give me enough to cover her expenses, and that's about it. But I love the dogs and enjoy the thought that, someday, she will be helping someone who can't see to have a fuller life."

"That does sound rewarding."

"It is," the trainer agreed. "They send me invitations to the graduation ceremonies for each puppy I've trained."

"Graduation?"

"Yes. When she's ready, Bessie will go to a training center where she'll be taught the skills needed to be a guide dog. Once she's mastered those, she'll be matched up with a blind person. Then, she and her new owner will train together. They'll get to know each other, eat together, sleep together, and work together under the supervision of skilled trainers; some blind, some sighted. When they've passed all the tests, they have a graduation ceremony. I love attending those. It makes me happy to see my puppies working with their new owners."

The rest of the bus ride, Frank and Carl talked about the other puppies he'd trained and experiences he'd had with each of them. When Frank reached his stop, he shook the trainer's hand.

"It's been a pleasure meeting you, Carl. I hope we meet again."

"As do I, Frank," Carl smiled.

Slogging his way to the machine shop, Frank wondered if he might explore this new occupation.

Then he grinned.

Nope, he thought, *a machinist doesn't have time to train puppies. Maybe when I retire.*

Chapter 2

"Come on, Frank!" his buddy, Steve, shouted at him. "Powder waits for no man!"

Frank grinned and finished strapping on his skis. It was a perfect ski day. Clear, sunny, and fresh-fallen snow. This was his first time skiing this year, money being tighter than usual, and he was looking forward to skiing the backside of the mountain. It always gave him a thrill to go where most skiers feared to tread.

He made his way to the lift and caught up with his friend. They chatted as they rode to the top, Frank admiring the view as he always did. The mountains looked so clean and white with their new coat of powdery snow. The pine trees created a stark contrast at the edges of the groomed runs.

When they reached the top, their skis hit the snow, and in unison, they stood up. The chairlift continued moving, giving them a little push away from the lift. Instead of turning right to follow the other skiers to the groomed runs, Frank and Steve veered left, heading for the "backside" of the mountain.

Standing at the top, Frank took a deep breath, feeling the cold air enter his lungs. He smiled when he breathed out, and a misty cloud left his nostrils, turning immediately into ice crystals glittering in the sun.

He adjusted his goggles, gripped his ski poles, and looked over at Steve, who was waiting for him.

"Ready?" he asked.

"Always," Steve replied as he pushed off and began his run down the pristine slope.

Frank followed, feeling the exhilaration of almost floating on the new powder. Skiing a groomed trail was fine. It was satisfying to hear your skis carving through the packed snow. But here, there was only silence as he slid over the snow. He knew the first cliff was just up ahead.

He loved to jump off the twenty-foot ledge, soaring through the air, and landing in the deep powder at the bottom. All he had to do was navigate the trees between here and there. Right around the first stand of trees, straight to the next, then left, crouch a little, and jump!

Except, he didn't turn left. Couldn't turn left. Bending his body and leaning in that direction didn't help, it just landed him on his side in the snow.

That was weird, he thought.

"Hey, Frank!" Steve called, shushing to a stop

and looking over his shoulder. "Did you decide to take a nap on me?"

"Nah," Frank called back. "Just wanted to see what the view was like from down here."

"Well, get up and let's get going," Steve insisted. "We've lost momentum for the first cliff. It's gonna be a lame jump, I'm afraid. Come on."

Frank struggled a little to get up but managed to regain his footing and took a deep breath.

"Last one over the cliff buys lunch!" he called as he skied past Steve.

Although he wasn't moving as fast as he might have if he hadn't fallen, the thrill was still there as his skis flew off the edge of the first cliff. Airborne, he couldn't help but yell, "Woohoo!"

Then, he hit the bottom, and his legs gave out. He crumpled and rolled in the deep powder, his eyes, nose, and mouth filling with snow. When he stopped rolling, he pushed over onto his back and sputtered a moment before taking several deep, gasping breaths.

"Did you forget to lift your tips?" Steve asked as he skied to a stop beside him.

"I guess," Frank replied, trying to return his breathing to normal. He sat up and looked up at his friend. "I'm not sure what happened there, to be honest."

"Don't worry about it," Steve said, holding out a helping hand. "Everybody falls from time to time. It's part of the fun."

Frank gripped it and pulled. When he was

standing upright again, he took stock of his limbs, poles, and skis. Nothing broken.

"Shake it off, man," Steve said. "We still have half a mountain left."

"Right," Frank replied.

Following Steve down the next section, Frank tried to ski like he normally did, but discovered that while right turns were easy, left turns were harder to navigate. It's almost as if he was turning through sand instead of snow. His body simply wouldn't make the left turns.

He managed to make it to the next cliff without falling over, but he could feel his legs shaking with the exertion. Determined to stay on his feet, he pushed hard and flew over the edge.

Again, the thrill of flying through the air filled him. It was tempered a bit, however, by his fear of the landing. Concentrating on keeping his tips up, he landed perfectly. Then, he turned left to see where Steve was. Rather, he *tried* to turn left, but landed face first in the snow again.

Steve landed a few yards away and skidded to a stop.

"What's wrong with you, Frank?" he asked. "You're skiing like a snow bunny today."

"I don't know," Frank replied, sitting up. "Just an off day, I suppose."

"Think you can make it to the highway?"

"Yeah. Not too many left turns between here and there, right?" Frank tried to joke.

"What?" Steve looked puzzled. "Left turns?"

Frank shook his head. "Never mind. You go on ahead. I'm going to take it a bit easier on this last leg."

Steve shrugged. "Suit yourself." He turned and pushed off, weaving his way expertly between the trees. Soon, even the powdery cloud of snow he'd created was gone from Frank's view.

Frank pushed himself to a standing position and surveyed the scene before him. It really was beautiful. Just trees, open spaces with deep snow, and nearly half a mile between here and the highway. No left turns? Not likely.

Slowly, Frank thrust his poles into the snow and felt his skis sliding forward. Trying to keep his speed down was hard. Trying to avoid left turns was harder. Several times, he found himself heading straight for a tree. Snowplowing his skis, he managed to slow enough to keep from hitting it full on, turning right at the last minute to scrape the trunk with his right shoulder. After the third one, Frank stopped and leaned against it, breathing hard.

What was wrong with him? This made no sense.

Standing straight, he kept one hand on the tree trunk and twisted his body to right. No problem. Then, he switched hands and twisted his body left. Still no problem.

Hm. He frowned, then did a little stretch one way, then the other. He bent his knees and tried to squat over his skis. Feeling his balance slipping, he quickly grabbed the tree again. Weirder and weirder.

Well, there was nothing he could do about it here. So, he continued his slow pace down the mountain, trying to avoid left turns whenever possible. As he broke through the tree line, he could see he was off course. Skiing straight towards the highway, he kept his eyes open for Steve. Finally, he spotted him, several hundred yards up the highway. He found a boulder on the side of the road, sat on it and removed his skis. Enough was enough.

By the time he'd finished, Steve had joined him.

"You sure took your sweet time coming down," his friend chided. "I turned down three rides before you showed up."

"Sorry," Frank said simply. "Just enjoying the view."

"Right," Steve responded sarcastically. "I'm guessing you don't want to make another run."

"You guess right. I think I'll call it a day. Maybe I'm coming down with something and just need a little rest."

"Maybe. I think I'll see if someone at the lodge wants to do a run with me. Can you get home okay?" Steve asked.

"No problem," Frank replied.

It didn't take long for Frank to find a way home. There were always skiers coming and going, and if someone had a free seat, they'd gladly offer it to another skier who needed a ride.

Frank rode in silence, worried about what he'd just experienced. But by the time they reached Pine Valley, he'd convinced himself that the excuse he'd given Steve must be true. He was coming down with something, and his body was too busy fighting it off to be bothered to ski correctly. A few days' rest, and he'd be right as rain again.

Chapter 3

A month later, the weather had turned icy again. Frank was grateful the line leading to the time clock hadn't stretched out the door into the freezing February air. When he reached the clock, Frank reached for his timecard. Oddly, as he went to grab it, it fluttered out of his hand and slid to the floor. Frowning, he bent down to pick it up.

"Fumble-fingers, today, Frank?" the burly man behind him teased.

Standing up, Frank tried to laugh it off. "Yeah, Dave, I just washed my hands and can't do anything with them."

The men in line laughed, but in his mind, Frank wasn't laughing. First, the fall at the bus stop, then his weird ski experience, now dropping his timecard. Something didn't feel right. He took a deep breath as he punched in, carefully returning the card to its slot.

The rest of the morning was uneventful. No

dropped parts or stumbling around in the machine shop, which was a good thing. Falling anywhere near those machines could be disastrous!

As he joined a couple of the other men heading back from the lunchroom, Frank joked and laughed with the rest. Unexpectedly, his boss, Vern Christiansen, came out of a side door. Frank sidestepped to avoid running into him and lost his balance. Trying to regain his footing, he took two huge sideways steps toward the wall, but it wasn't enough.

"Oomph!" Frank grunted as his shoulder slammed into the concrete wall with a loud thud.

Most of the men laughed, but Vern was quiet, merely reaching out a hand to him. Frank accepted it with a nod of thanks.

"What was in that soda you had for lunch?" one of the men joked. "Sneaking in booze, are you?"

Frank tried to laugh it off as he rubbed his shoulder. He stretched it forward and backward, then shrugged it in a circle. No harm done, it seemed.

Vern watched, his expression speculative. "Hey, Berglund, walk down the hall for me."

"Sir?" Frank eyed his boss with trepidation. "Why?"

"Humor me," Vern instructed.

Frank took a deep breath, then strode off down the hall… but his gait was anything but straight. He wandered from one side of the hall to the other and back. When he turned, he nearly lost his balance again, but managed not to fall this time.

When he reached Vern and the other men, no one was laughing. Looking into their faces, Frank felt a need to defend himself.

"That run-in with the wall must have shaken me up more than I thought," he laughed weakly.

Vern looked thoughtful for a moment. "I want you to stop by my office before you return to work, Berglund. I have a phone call to make, so give me five minutes."

"Yes, sir." Frank tried to sound more confident than he felt.

Nodding at the men, Vern strode down the hall in the direction of the offices.

Frank expected the guys to rib him about the boss calling him on the carpet, but they were uncharacteristically silent. As they returned to the machine shop to work, Frank headed for the boss's office.

Vern looked up as he came in, then motioned for Frank to sit as he finished up his phone call.

Frank sat, but he certainly didn't feel very comfortable. He had a good relationship with his boss, and never minded talking with him about the job or other related topics. But for some reason he couldn't quite put a finger on, his stomach was tied up in knots this time.

"That's right," Vern said into the phone. "We'll arrange delivery for next week." Pause. "Great. Thanks, Paul."

Vern hung up the phone and sat back. He eyed Frank with an open air of concern.

"I'm worried about you, Berglund," he stated bluntly. "I've been noticing some unusual behaviors that make me wonder."

"Are you talking about my little joke in the hall, sir?" Frank asked, trying to make light of the situation.

Vern frowned. "Don't try to play me, son. That was no joke, and you know it."

Frank sighed but chose not to respond. What could he say, after all? He didn't know why he'd suddenly started dropping things and walked like he was three sheets to the wind.

"I want you to see a doctor," his boss continued. "Start with this ear, nose, and throat guy. It may be as simple as an inner ear infection."

Eyebrows raised, Frank accepted the card Vern handed him. "Inner ear? That could explain it, couldn't it?"

"It could," Vern nodded, "but if that's not it, I want you to keep searching until you find an answer. I'm putting you on administrative leave until we know what's causing this."

"What?" Frank was shocked. "You're laying me off?"

The boss shook his head. "No, I'm just saying don't come back to work until you're safe to be in the shop."

Frank sighed. He hadn't been willing to admit that something was *that* wrong, but in his heart, he'd felt *something* wasn't right.

"I'm on it," he replied, trying to put his signature phrase to good use here.

"You'd better be," Vern said sternly, then his features relaxed. "You're a good employee, Berglund. I don't want to lose you, and I don't want you to lose a finger or worse because of your health. Got it?"

Nodding, Frank felt chastised and valued at the same time. "Yes, sir. I'll take care of it."

"Good. I'll look forward to seeing you back here soon." With that, Vern reached for the phone again.

Frank recognized the unspoken dismissal. He stood and turned to leave, taking time to move carefully. As he left the shop, he glanced down at the card Vern had handed him. Shocked, he stopped and read it again.

Peter Conners, PhD
Ear, Nose, and Throat
555-135-2435
284 S. Main St.
Pine Valley, ID

Chuckling, he made his way to the bus stop. He'd known his neighbor was a doctor, but he hadn't known he was an ENT specialist. Suddenly, Frank felt much better. Peter would find the answer and get him fixed up. There was nothing to worry about.

Chapter 4

Mandy Irwin shivered as she pulled her coat tighter around her. She knew she lived in the mountains now, but the first day of March wasn't supposed to be this cold, was it? It should feel more like spring, to her way of thinking. Coming from Florida, anything below seventy degrees felt downright frigid!

She laughed to herself as she approached the clinic door, blinking her doe-brown eyes against a sudden gust of wind. Cold or not, she was grateful to have finally landed a job, and this one felt like a perfect fit.

She stopped, took out her new Kodak camera, and snapped a picture of the sign next to the front door.

Pine Valley Clinic
284 S. Main St.
Pine Valley, ID

Mom'll love this, she thought with a grin. A real job in a real clinic! When she'd finished her physician's assistant training in Florida, she'd searched for a job for several months. She had become quite discouraged and wondered if the technical college had sold her on a bogus career. They'd said that PAs were in demand and that she'd have no trouble landing a job when she finished their course.

But then she'd graduated, and no one came knocking down her door offering her a PA position. In fact, her mother had begun suggesting she apply for other work... like Wal-Mart, or McDonald's. How insulting! But now, here she was, about to embark on her new career in a successful clinic in Pine Valley, Idaho.

With a smug smile, the twenty-two-year-old slipped her phone in her bag and opened the door. Stepping inside, she removed her new hand-knit beanie, freeing her long brown hair. She shook it out, and ran her fingers through each side, flipping it behind her shoulders. Now, she was ready.

The waiting room was small, but clean and tidy, with chairs and benches along the walls with a double row in the middle, their backs touching.

Her first thought was, *Looks like someone's planning to play Musical Chairs after work.*

She stifled a giggle as she approached the desk.

A red-haired woman who appeared to be in

her mid-forties looked up and smiled. "We're not open yet, dear, but if you'll tell me your name, I can get your file ready while you're waiting."

"Oh, I don't have an appointment…" Mandy replied, returning her smile.

The receptionist's pleasant expression dimmed a little. "Oh, dear. We are terribly busy this week with that nasty flu going around, but let me see if we have an opening…"

"No, no," Mandy laughed. "I'm not a patient. I'm the new physician's assistant. I believe I'm supposed to report to Dr. Conners."

"Forgive me, dear," the receptionist's smile grew again. "We have so few new employees that I just assumed… Well, never mind. I'll let Dr. Conners know you're here. Welcome to Pine Valley!"

"Thank you."

A few minutes later, a short, stocky man with salt-and-pepper hair stepped around the corner. Spotting her, he grinned and held out his hand.

"Peter Conners. You must be Mandy Irwin." His greeting was friendly, and Mandy immediately felt comfortable.

"I am. It's a pleasure to meet you, Dr. Conners."

"Please, call me Peter," he invited. "No one around here calls me doctor."

Mandy's eyebrows raised. "Really? Why's that?"

"Probably because I grew up in Pine Valley.

Most of the older folks remember when I threw baseballs through their windows, or toilet-papered their trees at Halloween. A troublemaker like me could never be a respectable doctor, right?" Peter laughed and shrugged. "I'm just an old-fashioned country doctor at heart, just like my father, and my grandfather before him."

"But you're an ENT, right? That's a far cry from country doctor," Mandy protested.

"Oh, honey," the receptionist chided from behind her desk. "You'd better lose those big city ideas, or you'll never make it around here."

"Now Mable, let's give Miss Irwin a chance, shall we?" Peter scolded, but his voice was tender. He turned back to Mandy. "Have you met my receptionist?"

"Not officially," Mandy answered.

"Then let me make the introductions officially," he grinned. "Mandy Irwin, I'd like you to meet Mable Conners, our receptionist and my wife."

"Oh!" Mandy's eyes widened, then she recovered and stepped forward, her hand out. "It's nice to meet you, Mrs. Conners."

"Good lord!" Mable rolled her eyes. "Do you think I'd allow you to call my husband Peter and then insist that you call me Mrs. Conners? Oh, no. I'm just plain Mable, honey, and I'll call you Mandy. Now that's settled, would you show her around, Peter? I have to get ready for the influx of patients we're expecting today."

"Yes, dear," Peter grinned. As he led Mandy out of the waiting room, he leaned closer and whispered, "A wise man once told me that if I want to keep my wife happy, I need to use those two words often."

Mandy stifled a giggle as he led her down the hall. "Who was that wise man? Your father?"

"Nope," Peter's grin broadened. "My father-in-law on our wedding day."

Mandy laughed aloud, then tried to focus on the tour, memorizing where everything was. The tour didn't take long, since it was a small clinic. With only three doctors and six exam rooms, there really wasn't much to see.

"Forgive me, Peter," Mandy observed when they'd reached the last exam room, "but why are there only three doctors in Pine Valley?"

"We don't really need more than three," he replied. "Old Doc Martin is our general family doctor. He sees nearly everyone at one point or another in their lives. Greg Harris is our orthopedist/rheumatologist. He sees the older folks, and the younger ones when they break a bone. And I handle the allergies, sinus infections, ear infections, things like that. Between the three of us, we can deal with just about anything that happens here."

"What about more serious cases, like cancer, operations, and such?"

"The really serious cases, we refer to the doctors in Boise. They have the knowledge and resources to handle them."

Mandy nodded. "I understand. So, what will my duties be?"

Peter laughed. "Whatever I ask you to do. And if you don't mind, I may loan you out to the other two doctors if they need you worse than I do."

"Okay…" Mandy replied, beginning to feel a bit nervous.

"How about we start with something easy," Peter suggested. "Go get me a cup of coffee, then make sure exam room two is ready for our first patient. I'd like you to sit in on that exam, just to get you acclimated."

Mandy laughed. "Ah, so one of my duties is to be your barista?"

Peter joined in her laughter. "Nothing so fancy. Just black coffee with one sugar."

"Got it, boss," she saluted as she left to find the coffee pot.

Frank sat nervously in the familiar waiting room. It hadn't changed much over the years. The scratched wooden floor, the mismatched chairs along the wall, the row of chairs in the middle, the toys in the corner where two little ones played, the bench nearby where their harried-looking mother sat watching them. It was a scene he recalled seeing many times as he'd come in as a child with sniffles, measles, a broken wrist, or a knot on his head from falling out of the oak tree in his yard.

He wasn't usually nervous when he came here. He knew the doctors and trusted them. But this time, it felt different. This time, he didn't know what was wrong. His mind had played through all sorts of scenarios last night as he lay in bed, not sleeping.

The scene from *Kindergarten Cop* played over and over in his head.

"It might be a tumor," the little boy had said.

"It's not a tumor," the undercover cop had gruffly replied.

The voice in his head always had Arnold Schwarzenegger's voice. It was funny the first few times, but after the twentieth time his mind played that scene, he felt irritated and nervous. What if it *was* a tumor?

"Frank Berglund?" a pretty young woman called from the doorway.

Frank stood up and approached her. "I'm Frank," he introduced himself, wondering why he didn't recognize her.

"If you'll follow me, please," she smiled and turned to precede him down the hall.

"Um, I haven't seen you here before. How long have you been working at the clinic?" Frank asked, partly because he was intrigued by her, and partly because he needed a distraction.

She laughed, and his heart skipped a beat. "Probably because I just started today."

"Oh? Where did you move from?"

"Florida," she answered as they reached the exam room. "If you'll have a seat on the table, I'll take your vitals."

He pulled off his coat and hung it on the wall hook. Then, he sat on the end of the exam table and held out his arm.

Mandy fastened the blood pressure cuff around his upper arm, placed the tips of the stethoscope in her ears and the chest piece in the crook of his elbow.

"How do you like Pine Valley?" Frank asked.

She frowned at him. "Shh, please."

He closed his mouth for a moment, then tried again, "I'll bet the weather here is a lot colder than Florida."

"Mr. Berglund…" she began.

"Frank."

"What?" She looked confused.

"Frank," he grinned. "You can call me Frank."

"Oh." For a moment she looked flustered. "Well, Frank, I'm trying to listen for your heartbeat, so I can read the dial and determine what your blood pressure is. I can't hear if you're talking."

Now it was Frank's turn to look flustered. "I'm so sorry. I'll be quiet."

She pumped up the cuff again, then listened intently as she gradually let the air out. After a moment, she smiled and allowed the cuff to deflate completely.

"Your blood pressure is elevated a bit, but not enough to worry about," she announced.

"I'm surprised," Frank responded, winking at her.

"Why?" she asked, apparently missing the wink as she recorded the numbers in his chart.

"With you in the room, I would have expected my blood pressure to be *highly* elevated."

Mandy looked stern. "Mr. Berglund…"

"Frank."

She sighed. "Frank, I'm trying to do my job here. Please refrain from flirting while I'm working."

"Does that mean I can flirt with you when you're off the clock?"

"I'm not sure it's professional to flirt with patients, even off the clock," she smiled.

"Too bad. You're going to have a lonely time of it, then," Frank put on his most forlorn expression.

"Why's that?"

"Because everyone in town is a patient here at one time or another," he pouted.

Just then, Peter knocked and entered the room.

"Good morning, Frank. What seems to be the problem today?" he asked without preamble.

"Hi, Pete. I seem to be having trouble with my balance. I wondered if it might be an inner ear infection," Frank replied.

"Well, let's take a look," Peter took out his otoscope and peered into Frank's ears, then into each nostril. He examined his eyes and mouth, then pursed his lips.

"I'm not seeing any redness or inflammation either in your ears or sinuses," he reported. "Let's see what it is you're referring to. Join me in the hall, will you?"

Once they were in the hallway, he instructed Frank to walk down the hall to the other end and back again. Frank did as he was told, feeling anxious as he listed a bit from one side to the other. He stumbled as he tried to turn too quickly at the end of the hall, but he managed stay upright and returned with only a couple of bumps against the left wall.

Peter looked serious as Frank approached him, then motioned for them to return to the exam room.

"So, what do you think, doc?" Frank asked, unable to quell the rising fear in his belly.

"I think we need another test, my friend," the doctor answered. "I'd like you to go into Boise for an MRI."

Frank frowned. "That sounds serious, Pete. What do you think I have?"

"I'm not willing to say just yet. I don't want to alarm you unnecessarily. I just want to rule out a couple of things."

"It might be a tumor," Frank intoned in his best little-kid voice.

Peter chuckled, and Mandy looked confused.

"It's not a tumor!" the doctor replied in his best Schwarzenegger imitation.

Frank laughed. "Not bad, Pete!"

He looked at Mandy and laughed harder. "I don't think your new assistant gets the joke."

"Not to worry," Peter replied. "I'll fill her in later. I'll call in an order for the MRI. They'll get in touch with you to set up the appointment. Then, I'll let you know the results. Meanwhile, try not to turn too fast or bump into any more walls." He turned to leave, then stopped and looked back at Frank. "Oh, and you're officially off work until we get this figured out, okay?"

Frank sighed. "I don't have a choice, do I?"

"I'm afraid not," Peter looked sympathetic, then left the room.

"So, Miss Irwin," Frank said, glancing at her nametag, then putting on his best company smile. "What time do you get off work?"

Mandy shook her head, but grinned. "I'm not ready to date the first patient I've seen since I moved here, Mr. Berglund."

"Frank," they said in unison, then both laughed.

Chapter 5

Frank was bored, and it was a feeling he was unaccustomed to. He'd always been a hard worker, creating things to do when he wasn't working. But since his trip into Boise for the MRI last week, he simply had no energy to create work for himself. It was all he could do to get out of bed to go to the bathroom. Most days, he'd managed to feed himself cereal or a peanut butter sandwich, but even that little effort exhausted him, and he'd spend the next couple of hours sleeping.

Although it was nearly noon, he was still in bed, trying to convince himself to get up and make a sandwich. He was tired. Tired of laying around. Tired of not having energy. Tired of staring at the four walls. He was sick and tired of being sick and tired.

Why hadn't he decorated his little house? At least then he'd have something to look at besides the cobwebs in the corner.

Get up, Frank, he told himself. Get your keister in gear and do *something* today!

He tried to sit up. His body felt like it weighed two tons. Slowly, he rolled to one side and tried to prop himself up on his elbow. Even that took a Herculean effort. Finally, he was able to push himself up and swing his legs off the edge of the bed. The soothing coolness of the hardwood beneath his feet was comforting. He closed his eyes, wiggled his toes, and sighed.

Okay, Berglund, he instructed himself again, stand up and walk like a man.

Carefully, he tried to stand, holding onto the nightstand for balance. He succeeded on the second try and mentally applauded himself.

Now, one foot in front of the other. Right foot. Left foot. He was far enough away that he knew he'd need to let go of the nightstand with his next step. He took a deep breath and…

CRASH!

His legs buckled, and he went careening to the floor, grabbing at anything within reach. Unfortunately, the first thing he grabbed was the lamp. Carrying it down with him, he heard the lightbulb shatter as the lampshade flew off into the corner.

He lay there for a moment, trying to catch his breath. That was new. He'd felt off-balance for a while now, but his legs had never buckled under him like that. When his heart had slowed its frantic beating, he rolled to his hands and knees, intending to try standing again. After a couple of failed attempts, he gave up and crawled to the bathroom.

A man's got to do what a man's got to do, he thought.

After struggling to accomplish his tasks in the bathroom, he slid to the floor and crawled out the door into his bedroom. As he rounded the corner, he noticed the phone lying on the floor beside the nightstand, the handset lying askew just under the bed. With great effort, he reached the phone, replaced the handset, and started to lift it up to the nightstand.

He dropped it when it immediately started ringing. Scowling at the offending telephone, he picked up the receiver and put it to his ear.

"Hello?"

"Frank?" It was Peter.

"Yes. Any word, Pete?"

"As a matter of fact, yes. Can you come into the office this afternoon?" Peter asked.

"Um," Frank looked at his legs and frowned, "I don't think so, Pete. I'm having a little trouble staying upright."

"Ooh. That bad, huh?"

"Yeah."

"Okay, buddy," Peter said reassuringly. "I'll come by later this afternoon to check you over and give you the MRI report."

"Why can't you give it to me over the phone? Am I dying?" Frank felt his heart start to race again.

"No, this isn't fatal, but I'd rather talk about it in person. That way, we can discuss treatment options and decide where we go from here, okay? I've got a patient waiting, so I'll see you later."

As the phone went dead in his hand, Frank was tempted to throw it across the room. He was more frustrated than he'd ever been in his life. Why couldn't Pete have just told him what the report said? This waiting hours after waiting days was going to drive him crazy!

He sighed, looked up at the bed and decided it was too much effort. He pulled at the blankets until they slid on top of him. Looking at his pillow longingly, he shook his head. Nope. Not worth the exertion. He gathered the blankets around him, bunching up one corner to serve as a makeshift pillow, then promptly fell asleep.

Several hours later, Peter and Mandy trudged through the early spring snow to Frank's front door.

Peter knocked, and they waited. And waited. And waited.

"He's not answering," Mandy observed unnecessarily. "What shall we do?"

"Not to worry." Peter leaned over and picked up a decorative ceramic frog from the corner of the porch. He reached into its large mouth and retrieved a key. Putting it into the lock, he turned it, then grinned at his assistant. "There are advantages to living next door to my patient."

Mandy chuckled as Peter opened the door.

"Frank?" he called. "Where are you, buddy?"

A muffled voice came from the bedroom.

Motioning for Mandy to follow him, the doctor made his way through the sparse but well-kept little house. They found Frank lying on the floor, a blanket drawn carelessly around him, the lamp laying off to the side with what looked like lightbulb glass scattered around it.

Rushing to his side, Peter's expression turned from friendly to concerned in a flash.

"What's going on, Frank?" he asked. "Why are you on the floor?"

"Duh!" Frank groused. "I thought I'd try a change of scenery. Why do you think I'm down here?"

Peter frowned. "I didn't know it had gotten this bad, bud. Let's get you up."

He helped Frank to a sitting position, bending his legs at the knees. Supporting his friend's back, he nodded at Mandy who bent down and hooked her elbow under Frank's right shoulder. Peter hooked his under the left and on the count of three, they lifted together. Unfortunately, their first try wasn't entirely successful as the blanket under Frank's feet slid on the hardwood floor. He landed with a thud back on the floor.

"That was a trial run, right?" the doctor tried

to sound jovial, but there was tension in his voice. "Let's move that blanket and try again."

After maneuvering the blanket out from under Frank, they lifted again. This time, they managed to get him on his feet, but it was evident that he didn't have the ability to stand on his own. Fortunately, he was close to the bed, so they were able to slide him the rest of the way, then they turned him and helped him sit down on the edge. At that point, Pete started to let go, but Frank immediately leaned to the left, nearly falling over.

"Whoa, hang on there, buddy. Are you trying to imitate the Leaning Tower of Pisa, or a tree falling in the forest?" Peter tried to joke.

Frank wasn't laughing. He growled and scowled as Peter and Mandy tried to help him turn and slide to a sitting position against the headboard. After a few awkward attempts, Frank told him in no uncertain terms that he was just fine where he was.

Mandy looked uncomfortable and asked, "Where's your broom, Mr.… uh, Frank?"

"Why?" he grumbled.

"I thought I'd clean up this glass before you cut yourself," she replied.

He motioned to the door and mumbled, "Hall closet."

"Thanks," she said as she went to retrieve the broom.

"Let's see what's going on here," Peter said reaching for his stethoscope. He listened to

Frank's heart, then looked in his eyes and ears.

Before he could check any further, however, Frank slapped his hand away. "Enough, Peter! Just tell me what the damned MRI said!"

Peter sat back and sighed. "I'm not going to sugarcoat it, Frank. The MRI shows you have multiple sclerosis lesions on your spinal column."

"What?" Frank looked shocked.

"Multiple sclerosis, often called MS," the doctor repeated.

Frank closed his eyes and leaned his head back against the headboard. After a few moments of silence, Mandy came back in. Peter looked up at her questioning expression and shook his head.

Finally, Frank returned his attention to Peter. "I've heard of MS, but I don't really know what that is. Could that be why I've been seeing double this past week?"

"Seeing double?" Peter repeated. "Let's take another look at your eyes."

Pulling his ophthalmoscope out of his bag, turned on the tiny light, and examined Frank's left eye, then his right.

"I'm not seeing anything abnormal, but perhaps a trip to the eye doctor would be in order," he suggested.

"Yeah, right," Frank responded with a huge helping of sarcasm. "I'll jump right out of this bed and dance my way there."

Peter frowned. "I'm sorry. I should be more sensitive. I do think once we get this in hand, you should really have your eyes examined."

"I'll get right on that," Frank said sourly. Then, he looked at Peter. "Look, Pete, I know I asked this before, but am I dying?"

"No. At least, not any faster than I am. Do you want the long explanation or the abridged version?"

"I'm not up for a long medical explanation, doc. Short and sweet, please."

"You got it. MS is an autoimmune disease where your body attacks the sheaths of the nerve cells in your brain and spinal cord."

Again, Frank frowned. "So, what does all that mean for me?"

"The truth?"

"Yes!"

"I don't know," Peter admitted.

"What do you mean you don't know?" Frank asked gruffly. "Are you a doctor, or aren't you?"

"Every patient is different. Apparently, your particular set of symptoms includes weakness, lack of balance, and an inability to support yourself in an upright position."

"Ya' think?" Frank scowled. "Tell me something I don't know!"

"Okay, from what I'm seeing today, I think we need to talk about getting you someplace where you can get the care you need."

Frank's eyes widened. "Care? A nursing home? I'm too young for a nursing home, Pete! You know that!"

"Age has nothing to do with it, Frank. Considering the position we found you in today, I think that's something you can't avoid. At least, not until you learn to fend for yourself better than this," Pete insisted, gesturing to the lamp Mandy was returning to the nightstand.

"No," Frank said flatly. "No way."

Peter frowned. "The only other option is to bring you a wheelchair and get a physical therapist to teach you how to transfer into and out of it. We should also probably look into an aid to come in a couple of times a week."

"What for?"

"To help you with those things you can't do for yourself, and to keep track of your vitals, that sort of thing."

Silently, Frank turned his face to the window.

"Shall I set it up?" Peter pressed.

"Whatever," Frank mumbled.

"All right, then. I'll make some calls and will let you know who to expect. Shall I tell them where the key is, or would you rather we install a lock box?"

"This is Pine Valley," Frank muttered. "Everyone knows where my key is."

Peter caught Mandy's expression out of the corner of his eye. She looked shocked. He knew he'd need to explain a few things to her later.

"Right." Peter stood and asked, "Would you like us to help you to a more comfortable position?"

Frank just shook his head.

"Okay. I'll stop by tomorrow and hope to have more info for you."

When Frank didn't answer, Peter motioned for Mandy to leave the room. When she was gone, he leaned over the bed.

"I know this is hard, Frank. Just hang in there, and we'll figure it out."

Frank didn't acknowledge that he'd heard a word. He just sat, silently staring out the window.

Met with only silence, Peter looked sadly at his friend. "See you tomorrow, Frank." When Frank remained silent, he joined Mandy at the front door.

As they left, Peter carefully locked the front door, then chuckled wryly at the expression on his assistant's face.

"You're wondering 'why lock the door'," he guessed.

"Yeah, if everyone knows where his key is, and if Pine Valley is so safe, why lock the door?"

Peter smiled sadly. "Truthfully, it's all for show. Nearly everyone knows where everyone else's spare key is, so logically, it doesn't make sense. But everyone feels safer when their doors are locked."

Mandy nodded, but looked perplexed.

"Not to worry," Peter patted her shoulder. "It's a small-town quirk."

Upstairs, Frank was staring out the window next to his bed. He'd put his bed there deliberately and had always enjoyed looking out when he woke up each morning.

Just now, he watched the neighbor boy shoveling snow. The boy finished his driveway and sidewalk, then looked over at the nearly pristine snow in Frank's driveway. He hesitated a moment, then continued shoveling the walk in front of Frank's house. When that was clear, he shoveled Frank's driveway, and finally, he shoveled the sidewalk leading to Frank's door.

Frank frowned. He should be doing that. It was *his* driveway. It was *his* front walk. It was *his* responsibility to keep it clear of snow. Frank felt the anger rise and build within him. It wasn't fair! It just wasn't fair! Without conscious thought, he formed his hands into fists and pounded the bed on either side of his body, yelling at the ceiling, throwing a full-blown temper tantrum at the unfairness of it all. When he'd run out of steam, which didn't take long, he drifted into a fitful sleep.

Chapter 6

The morning air was crisp as Mandy pulled the wheelchair out of her car. She noticed the driveway had been shoveled since they'd been here yesterday and mentally thanked the good Samaritan for keeping her from slipping on the ice that seemed to be everywhere. She'd been concerned about that when Peter had asked her to check on Frank.

Did they often have snow and ice in March here? She'd have remember to ask someone.

Wheeling the chair up to the front door, she frowned at the two steps leading to the small porch. That would be a problem when Frank was ready to maneuver the chair out of his little house. Mental note: talk to Peter about having someone install a ramp.

She knocked out of courtesy, then retrieved the key from the frog's mouth, returning it after the door was unlocked.

"Frank?" she called as she entered. There was no response.

As she pushed the empty chair into the bedroom, she put on her most cheerful voice.

"Good morning, Frank. How are you this morning?"

Frank just groaned a little.

"I've brought you a wheelchair. The physical therapist will be by a bit later to show you how to transfer from the bed into the chair."

Again, Frank groaned. He shifted a bit in the bed and opened one eye. "Whryhr?" he mumbled.

"Pardon?" Mandy stepped closer to the bed.

"Why… are… you… here?" Frank asked again, more clearly this time.

"I'm here to check on you and bring you the wheelchair you'll be using," she replied smiling.

"I don't want a wheelchair," Frank grumbled.

Mandy leaned in a whispered, "No one does." She straightened up and grinned. "At least, no one that I've ever met."

Frank grunted.

"Would you like me to help you sit up?" she asked.

Shaking his head, Frank turned his face to the window.

"Have you had breakfast? I could whip up some eggs, if you'd like."

Again, Frank shook his head.

Mandy frowned. "When was the last time you ate?"

"Not hungry," her patient muttered.

"I can understand that, but you need to eat to keep your strength up. You'll need it."

"For what? I'm not going anywhere," Frank groused.

"Perhaps not yet," she tried to keep her voice cheerful, but felt herself becoming irritated with his rude and defeatist attitude. "But soon, you'll be wheeling yourself anywhere you'd like to go. The physical therapist will teach you how to transfer and the most efficient ways to maneuver the chair around obstacles. It will…"

"Stop! Just stop!" Frank exploded.

Mandy's eyes widened. "What?"

"Stop with the phony cheerfulness and counterfeit kindness. Don't you get it? I don't want a wheelchair. I don't want breakfast. I don't want you to help me in any way. Most of all, I don't want your simulated sunny smiles trying to cheer me up! Just leave… me… alone!"

Several expressions crossed Mandy's face as she listened to her patient's tirade. Mentally, she knew where his anger was coming from and that it wasn't truly about her. It was a normal reaction to the diagnosis and stemmed from his feelings of helplessness. Most men hated that feeling, and she sensed that Frank was an intensely independent person.

However, Mandy had never taken well to being verbally attacked, even when she understood the provocation. She gritted her teeth, trying to keep her own anger from surfacing. She was a professional, after all. It wouldn't do to lose control with a patient, especially one who was lying helplessly in bed, unable to do much for himself.

That thought softened her mindset, and she was able to reassert her professional demeanor. "Be that as it may, Mr. Berglund," she stated matter-of-factly. "I have a job to do, and part of that job is to see that your physical needs are met. I'll refrain from excessive cheerfulness if that will make you more comfortable. But I *will* do my job, and if you want to request someone else to help you, be my guest. Meanwhile, let's get down to business."

With only that cryptic warning, she stepped forward and pulled the blanket and sheets back, revealing that Frank did, indeed, have a situation that needed immediate attention. She glanced at his horrified expression, then set about cleaning him up. He threw dark looks her way as she worked, but she didn't even glance at his face, focusing entirely on the task before her.

When he was once again in fresh pajamas, lying on fresh sheets, she finally looked at him.

"Mr. Berglund, would you prefer eggs or cereal this morning?"

"I'm not…"

"I don't care, Mr. Berglund. If you have no preference, I will make you some eggs and toast. Then, I will stay to ensure that you eat. When I am satisfied that you have enough nutrition in you to withstand the physical therapy you're about to undergo, then, and only then, will I leave you alone. That is, until tomorrow, when we will do this all over again, hopefully without the attitude." Mandy's tone was no-nonsense, perfectly professional, but brooked no argument.

Frank's jaw dropped.

She didn't give him time to answer, however, as she turned on her heel and left the room.

Once she was safely in the kitchen, she leaned against the counter, taking deep, shaky breaths. She shouldn't cry. She couldn't cry. She wouldn't cry! She refused to allow him to see how much his unspoken pain affected her. If he knew she was vulnerable to his outbursts, there would be no end to it. She had to maintain her professional demeanor, at least until he accepted his diagnosis and was willing to be more cooperative.

Her emotions back under control, she quickly whipped up some scrambled eggs, toast, and coffee. As she cooked, her mind wandered back to when her mother was first diagnosed with MS. Mandy recalled the all-out temper tantrums, the sullen silences, the lack of cooperation. It was a hellish time for the entire family.

The night her father left, taking her six-year-old brother with him, Mandy thought life was over. She was only thirteen years old! How was she supposed to care for her invalid mother by herself?

The image of their kindly neighbor flashed into her mind. Mrs. Thornton. The sweetest, most giving woman on the planet. Without her help and support, Mandy was sure she would have ended up in foster care, and her mother would have been placed in a nursing home.

May heaven bless that woman from here to eternity, Mandy thought.

When the eggs were done and the toast buttered, she looked for a tray to carry the breakfast on. Finding no tray, she settled for the broiler pan she found in the drawer under the oven.

Stopping just outside the bedroom door, she took a deep breath, plastered her best professional no-nonsense expression on her face, then pushed the door open with her hip. She placed the pan on the nightstand, then helped Frank to a more upright position, leaning against the headboard with pillows behind his back.

"Shall I feed you?" she asked, knowing he wouldn't take kindly to that suggestion.

She was right.

"I can manage," he responded, his voice still angry, but subdued.

Mandy wandered around the room, picking up a few things that had fallen on the floor, placing the soiled clothes in the hamper, filling his glass with water, and generally trying to look busy as she made sure he ate.

Finally, he dropped his fork noisily onto the plate.

"Will you please sit down?" he asked,

obviously irritated. "You're driving me crazy."

"As you wish, Mr. Berglund," she acquiesced.

Sitting on a folding chair in the corner, she tried hard not to stare at him as he picked up his fork and resumed eating. She looked at the floor, examined a picture on the wall across from her, and finally settled on staring out the window.

"Why am I suddenly 'Mr. Berglund' again?" Frank finally asked.

She couldn't help it; she smiled, then a giggle bubbled up from somewhere inside. The giggle turned into a laugh, which became quite uncontrollable. It was probably a reaction to the tenseness of the situation, her analytical side observed.

I really should stop, Mandy thought, as she watched her patient staring at her, bewilderment on his face. But still, the laughter continued, uncontrolled.

Gradually, Frank's expression morphed from confusion, to a small smile, then a little grin, then a chuckle, and ultimately, he was laughing along with her.

When her sides hurt, and her cheeks ached from the almost hysterical mirth, she finally regained control and wiped her eyes with the tissue she pulled from her pocket.

"I'm sorry, Frank." She offered him a genuine smile. "I don't mean to be insensitive, and I hope you'll forgive me."

Frank shook his head. "No apology

necessary. I've been a real jerk, and I'm sorry."

"Shall we start again, then?" Mandy asked.

"Yes, please," he grinned.

"So, there will be no request for another aide?" she teased.

"No. I'd like you to stay on, if you're willing," he responded contritely. "I promise to try and behave like a civilized human being."

"It's a deal," she nodded, standing.

Reaching for the broiler pan, she asked, "You don't happen to have a serving tray, do you?"

"No. That's not something a bachelor needs very often."

"I'll bring one tomorrow," she smiled and turned to go. When she reached the door, she looked back. "I'll make a sandwich for you and leave it in the refrigerator. Just have your physical therapist grab it for you before he leaves. I believe Peter has arranged for someone to bring in some dinner for you."

"That isn't n…"

"Necessary?" she interrupted. "Of course, it is. You'll need your…"

"…strength," he finished for her, grinning.

That's better, Mandy thought as she made her way back into the kitchen. Quickly making a sandwich and cleaning up the dishes, she found herself humming. *So much nicer when he's pleasant,* she thought.

She gathered her things and opened the front door, then jumped a little as a tall, thin man stepped onto the porch.

"Oh, I'm sorry," he offered. "I didn't mean to startle you."

Mandy smiled. "That's okay. I just didn't expect to see you there. I'm Mandy Irwin, Frank's aide."

"Nice to meet you, Mandy. I'm Kevin Sawyer, Frank's physical therapist."

"Oh, good. I've got him all warmed up for you," she grinned.

Kevin's eyebrows rose as she brushed by him and made her way down the walk.

"Warmed up?" he called after her.

"Ask *him* about that!" she called back, laughing.

Frank watched out the window as Mandy climbed into her car.

She certainly has a way of cutting through the crap, he thought. He heard Kevin come in but didn't turn to look. After Mandy's car drove out of sight, he finally acknowledged his friend's entrance.

"She's quite the lady, isn't she," Kevin remarked.

Frank grinned. "She certainly is."

Kevin cocked his head. "You seem to be in better spirits than I expected. Could it be the cute new aide has made you forget your troubles? Peter told me you were having a hard time adjusting to this new development."

Frank's expression turned sour. "New development? Is that what he's calling it?"

"What would you call it?" Kevin asked.

"I guess that's as good a label as any," Frank scowled, looking out the window again.

Kevin glanced toward the wheelchair. "Shall we get started?"

"Started?" Frank asked, not turning his head.

"With your physical therapy," Kevin answered.

Puzzled, Frank tore his eyes away from the blobs of melting snow falling from the tree outside. "What?"

"I'm your physical therapist."

"Wait, I didn't know you were a physical therapist. We've known each other for how long? Why didn't I know this?"

Kevin laughed. "You never asked. I don't think we've ever discussed our work. We always find more interesting things to talk about."

Frank thought for a moment, then nodded. "I guess you're right." He sighed. "I don't know what you think you can do with me. I'm pretty much useless these days."

"So I hear," Kevin concurred. "But that's my job. I take useless muscles and teach them to be useful again," the therapist grinned as he stepped forward.

The next half hour was grueling as Kevin pushed and pulled and twisted Frank's feet, legs, hips, and back. It wasn't exactly painful, but it was certainly not comfortable as he felt his limbs moving in ways he didn't know were possible. All the while, Kevin kept up a light banter, alternating between explaining what he was doing, and distracting Frank with idle chit-chat.

Finally, when Frank was sure he couldn't take any more, Kevin stepped over to the wheelchair.

"Now for some fun," he announced.

"Fun?" Frank asked suspiciously.

"Sure!" Kevin smirked. "So far, I've been doing all the work. Now, it's your turn."

"What are you expecting me to do, Kevin? In case you hadn't noticed, my legs are non-functional."

"Perhaps, but your arms are still strong, and your back is strong. It's just not getting the signals you need from your brain to keep you upright. So, I'm going to teach you how to use the strength in your arms and back to transfer from the bed into the wheelchair. Once you've mastered that, I'll teach you how to maneuver around. Then, the whole world will open up for you. Not only will you be able to get out of that bed, but you'll have the ability to go anywhere you want."

Frank frowned. "I find that hard to believe. How am I supposed to get out my door and down my front steps? I can't drive anymore. How am I supposed to go anywhere? Even if my arms are still strong, I'm pretty sure I can't wheel myself across town."

"Not yet, no," Kevin agreed. "However, as you know, Pine Valley has a very good bus system. You also know that it's fare-free, so you don't even need to carry change! As for the rest, one step at a time, my friend."

"Step?" Frank scowled.

Kevin laughed. "Sorry, Frank. Slip of the tongue there."

He brought the wheelchair next to the bed, raised the armrest closest to the bed, and locked the brakes.

"Now," he instructed, "I'll brace your back so you're sitting upright. I want you to swing your legs over the side of the bed."

"You're kidding, right?" Frank asked, incredulous.

Kevin looked his friend in the eyes. "I'm serious, Frank. As your friend, I refuse to let you wither away in this bed for the rest of your life. You have too much to give this world."

"Like what?"

"Your heart, Frank," Kevin replied sincerely. "You have the most giving heart of anyone I've ever met."

"Had," Frank muttered sullenly.

Kevin cocked his head. "I don't believe that. I believe you'll find a way to give again."

"Yeah? How?"

"I don't know. But I do know that you can't keep a good man down, and you're a good man. So, let's work together and get you out of that bed."

Frank still looked dubious, but didn't argue, so Kevin moved to the head of the bed behind the wheelchair. He helped Frank sit up, bracing his back as he struggled. When he was sitting mostly upright, Kevin continued the instructions.

"Now, slide your legs off the side."

Frank pushed with all his might, but only managed to move his legs a few inches.

"It's no use," he said, leaning back against Kevin's hands. "I don't get it. It was easier yesterday. I even walked a few steps just yesterday. Why can't I move them today?"

"MS is a tricky disease," Kevin replied. "One day, you'll have a little control, the next, it'll be gone. Tomorrow, it may be back again." Kevin pursed his lips thoughtfully. "Okay, let's try something else. Try grabbing the fabric on the right leg of your pajamas at the knee. Lift your leg using the fabric. When you can, slide your left hand under your knee and use that to help slide your leg off."

With a sigh of resignation, Frank followed Kevin's directions. It worked! He let out a victory whoop when his foot fell over the side of the bed.

"Great! Good work," Kevin praised. "One more time with your left leg."

Again, success!

"That's incredible!" Frank exclaimed.

Kevin chuckled. "Nice work, but you're not there yet. With your right hand, reach over to the armrest farthest away from you. Your left hand will brace behind you on the bed keeping you upright. When both hands are in position, push up with your arms and swing your body to the right. If all goes well, your butt will slide off the bed and into the chair. Ready?"

Frank took a deep breath and nodded. "Ready."

He placed his left hand on the bed behind him, took another deep breath, then leaned over to grab the armrest on the wheelchair. He nearly lost his balance and was grateful that Kevin was holding on to him. With Kevin's support, he was able to reach the armrest. Leaning his weight on that side, he took another deep breath, pulled with his right hand and pushed with his left. Miraculously, his body swayed and slid from the bed to the chair.

Too out of breath to cheer, Frank just grinned over at his friend.

"Nicely done!" Kevin exclaimed as he applauded. "Not many can do that on the first try. We'll want to strengthen your arms and back even more so you can do that without help, but it's a great start!"

Frank didn't reply. He just sat, breathing hard and wondering how he would ever be able to do that without Kevin to support him.

Still, Kevin wasn't through.

"Okay, buddy," he said in his no-nonsense therapist voice. "Now, you have to get back."

"What?!"

Frank was in shock. He didn't think he could even move, let alone move his dead-weight body back to the bed.

"You can do it," Kevin encouraged. "Just reverse the movement. Push with your right hand, lean on your left, then slide your body over."

The return trip was definitely harder. The mattress was soft, so it didn't offer as much support for holding the weight of his body. Still, after several unsuccessful attempts, he managed to slide a little, and finally roll onto the bed. Kevin helped him straighten out and lay back on the pillows.

Frank's arms felt like jelly, and his back was screaming from the unaccustomed exertion.

Kevin opened his mouth, but Frank cut him off. "Enough, Kevin! I can't do one more thing!"

"Fair enough," his friend replied. "We'll call it a day. But I want you to think about how far you've come. This morning, you couldn't even get out of bed to use the restroom."

Frank made a face. "I can't even imagine how I could manage that, even if I can get into the chair!"

"I've got that all arranged," Kevin chuckled. "Tomorrow, we'll install grab bars in the bathroom that will make it much easier for you."

"If you say so," Frank sighed. "Right now, I just want to sleep for a year."

"You've earned a rest," the physical therapist

agreed. "I'll make you some lunch and set it on the nightstand for you. I don't want you trying the transfer without someone here until you're more proficient at it, okay?"

"Mandy made a sandwich for me. It's in the fridge," Frank explained, his voice soft and weary.

"I'll get it," Kevin said.

Frank nodded sleepily. Two breaths later, a soft snore punctuated his exhalation.

Kevin grinned. As he turned to go, he noticed the wheelchair in arm's reach of the bed.

Best not leave temptation so close, he thought. Kevin wheeled the chair to the far corner of the room, glanced at his sleeping friend, then quietly left the room.

Chapter 7

One week later, Frank took a deep breath and rolled onto his side. Pushing himself up to a sitting position, he slid his legs off the side of the bed. Following the instructions Kevin had given him, he grabbed the arm of the wheelchair to start the transfer.

He couldn't help but grin as he slid successfully into the chair without mishap. It wasn't the first time he'd done it successfully, but it was the first time without Kevin to back him up.

I'm really getting good at this, he thought as he wheeled into the kitchen to fix himself some breakfast. He'd been wanting to fix his own breakfast for three days and felt quite proud of what he'd accomplished in only a week.

Deciding he wanted a heartier breakfast than the toast and coffee he'd originally planned, he opened the refrigerator and reached for the eggs. Pulling them out, he lost his grip and dropped the carton. It bounced off the arm of the wheelchair, then the wheel. By the time it hit the floor, the lid was open, and eggs were free-falling. Splat! Splat! Splat!

Frank frowned. Now he wasn't going to have eggs for breakfast, and he had a mess to clean up. Looking around the kitchen, he spotted the broom in the corner. That would only spread the slime around. Paper towels would work, but he couldn't reach the floor with them from his wheelchair. Hm. Maybe he'd ask Mandy to clean it up when she came later. No, by then, it would be a rock-hard blob. He sighed, then had an idea.

He wheeled over and picked up the broom and dustpan, laying the dustpan in his lap and propping the broom up on the footrest with the handle leaning against his shoulder. Carefully, he reached for the paper towels and laid them beside the dustpan.

Slowly, he wheeled back to the broken eggs. He wrapped the dustpan in paper towels, crimping the edges over the handle. Repeating the process with the broom, he now had tools he hoped would work. Dropping the dustpan on the floor, he used the towel-covered broom to maneuver it next to the eggs. Then, he lifted one leg up with his hands, pushed the footrest up, and allowed that foot to drop next to the handle of the dustpan.

Now comes the tricky part, he thought. Carefully, he placed the brush of the broom on the opposite side of the eggs and pulled. He nearly cheered when the slimy mess began to slide toward the dustpan. Fifteen minutes later, he felt reasonably satisfied that he had most of the eggs swept into the dustpan.

Now what? He couldn't reach the pan to pick it up. He couldn't empty it. Again, he thought about leaving it for Mandy. At least, if it hardened in the dustpan, the paper towels should be easy to slide into the trash can.

Having decided that, he wheeled to the trash can and pulled the slime-covered paper towel off the broom. He only got a little on himself. With that accomplished, he couldn't decide whether to go back to bed or fix himself toast and coffee.

No, he thought, *I want eggs!* He looked at the front door and made a monumental decision. There was a convenience store only a block from his house. He could wheel that far and buy some eggs, couldn't he?

With a determined expression, he grabbed his coat off the hook by the door and put it on. He opened the door and was faced with another challenge. The front steps. Frank scowled. Two steps stood in the way of a delicious egg breakfast!

After only a moment's hesitation, he reached for the wheels, leaned back as far as he could, and pushed.

The next few seconds were horrific as the wheelchair bumped, bounced, and finally landed on its side at the bottom of the steps. Frank landed on his face in the snow.

Lifting his head, he sputtered and tried to lift his hand to wipe the snow off his face. The moment he rolled a bit to free his arm, pain shot down his right leg. A moan escaped his lips as he lost consciousness.

After eight days in the hospital, Frank was more than ready to leave. Oh, the staff was wonderful and treated him with great respect and gentleness. But he'd never been one to stay still for long. Now that his broken hip didn't hurt quite so much, he was ready to get back to familiar surroundings and a little privacy.

He looked up when Peter came in.

"Good morning, doc," Frank greeted him with a smile. "Can I get out of here today?"

"That depends," Peter responded. "How's the hip this morning?"

"I'm ready to rumble! Bring it on!"

"I think you're snowing me just a bit," the doctor grinned, "but I like your enthusiasm. Let's take a look."

After a brief examination, Peter nodded. "Good news. I will release you today."

"Great!"

"I'll make arrangements for transportation to Shady Pines this afternoon."

"Shady Pines!" Frank exploded. "No way! I don't need a nursing home, Pete. I can manage just fine at home."

Peter shook his head. "I don't think so. You need to keep that hip as still as possible, and that's not going to happen if you're by yourself. In fact, being home alone is what got you into this predicament in the first place."

"I promise to be good," Frank pledged in his best little boy whine.

"No," the doctor's voice was as firm as any parent's. "When the hip is fully healed and you've proven you can really take care of yourself, we'll talk again."

Frank opened his mouth to protest, but Peter held up a hand stopping him.

"If all goes well, it will only be a couple of months. You can handle it for that long, can't you?"

Scowling, Frank bit back the retort that threatened to escape. When his friend got that parental tone in his voice, there was no changing his mind.

"Fine. But I don't have to like it."

"No, you don't," Peter chuckled. "But I think you'll manage better if you change that negative attitude just a bit. Open your mind and heart, Frank. You may be surprised at what you'll discover while you're there."

"Yeah, yeah," Frank groused.

Shaking his head, Peter smiled. "Try to get a little rest before your ride gets here. You'll be awfully tired after this change of venue."

"Whatever." Frank turned his head toward the window, hoping his friend would take the hint.

He did, leaving the room quietly and closing the door behind him.

Frank couldn't believe it. A nursing home! He was twenty-seven years old and going to live in a nursing home. That's where old people go to die! He sighed. Well, maybe that's it. Maybe he was going to check out of this life early. Might as well. He certainly wasn't much good in this condition, and a nursing home was as good as anyplace to wait for the inevitable, wasn't it?

Later that afternoon, Frank woke up in an unfamiliar room, a curtain drawn around his bed. It took a moment for him to remember where he was. Shady Pines Nursing Home. The place he would live out the rest of his days, which hopefully wouldn't be very long.

Peter had been right. He was exhausted! Even after a nap, he felt tired and weak. And his hip hurt! He frowned. When did he last have his pain meds? He couldn't remember, so he looked for a call button. Feeling around, he couldn't find one anywhere. There was nothing hanging from the railing on the bed. It didn't seem to be tucked under his arm. He even tried to roll a bit to feel under his back.

He screamed as the movement caused excruciating pain to radiate from his hip down his leg. Clamping his jaw, he gently returned to his previous position just as the curtain was pulled back, revealing an elderly man leaning on a walker.

"Are you all right, young man?" he asked in a quivery voice.

"Do I sound like I'm all right?" Frank responded through gritted teeth.

"Can't say that you do," the visitor replied honestly. "Why don't you call the nurse?"

Frank glared. "That's what I was trying to do. Can't find the blasted call button!"

"Ah," the man said with a knowing nod. "That gets everyone the first time." He slid his walker up to the side of the bed and pointed to the panel on the bedrail. "They got these newfangled contraptions a few months ago. Supposed to make it easier to call the nurses, since the call button never gets lost. But if they don't tell you where it is, how're you supposed to find it?"

With a raised eyebrow, Frank looked where he was pointing and asked, "So, where is it exactly?"

"Right here," the man said, pointing to a bump on the panel with an orange box sporting a white plus-sign. Above it, in tiny black letters, Frank could make out the word "Nurse".

He reached out and pressed it, and a little orange light came on. He looked up at the old man, "How long before they answer?"

"Depends on how busy they are. I'm Mike Hamblin, your roommate."

Roommate? He had a roommate?

When he didn't answer, Mike chuckled again.

"They didn't tell you, did they? That's okay. I promise to be as quiet as I can, so I don't disturb you. I generally spend my waking hours reading, and that's pretty quiet. Except when I drop my book. I do tend to snore a bit when I'm sleeping, but I'll do my best to keep it down. Oh, and I sometimes sing to myself when I'm feeling low. Music really helps with depression, don't you think?"

Was this what life was going to be like? Twenty-four-seven with a talkative old man, nurses who don't answer, and pain every time he moved? Unbearable!

"Just leave me alone!" Frank growled and closed his eyes. "Can't you see I'm in pain?"

Silence.

After a few moments, Frank opened his eyes. Mike was looking at him with great concern.

"Is there something I can do to help?" he asked softly.

His voice sounded sincere, which caught Frank off-guard. Taking a moment to really look at his new roommate, he saw gentleness in his blue eyes, unruly white hair, a salt-and-pepper beard where a few breadcrumbs nested, a rumpled plaid shirt, pajama bottoms, and blue-veined hands with fingers twisted with arthritis. The old man looked like he should be in bed asking for help himself!

A twinge of regret pricked at Frank's heart.

"I'm sorry… Mike, was it?"

The old man smiled. "Yup. Mike Hamblin."

"I'm sorry, Mike," Frank repeated. "I shouldn't be yelling at you. You're only trying to help."

"I understand," Mike replied. "The first few days are the hardest. Then, you get used to the routine and the people, and it's not so bad."

"What can I do for you, Mr. Berglund?" the nurse asked as she came in.

"I'll leave you to it, then," Mike said. "I'll be back later." He waved before he turned and shuffled out the door.

Chapter 8

"Are you sure?" Mandy asked skeptically. "Frank doesn't strike me as the kind to simply lie around just resting for six weeks."

Peter laughed. "Oh, he'll grouse about it, no doubt, but after he realizes he has no choice, he'll adjust and figure out a way to make it bearable. In fact, it wouldn't surprise me if he doesn't help someone along the way."

"Really? This is an awfully big adjustment."

"True. But you don't know Frank like I do. He's never been one to stay down for long," Peter reassured her.

Mandy nodded and turned back to her papers, but her mind wasn't on the work on her desk. It was on a certain patient stuck in a nursing home against his will.

When her workday ended, Mandy decided to pay a call to that patient. She couldn't help it. Frank Berglund had gotten under her skin, and she had to know if he was okay. As she drove from the clinic to Shady Pines, she waffled. Maybe he wouldn't want to see her. After all, there was surely a competent staff at the nursing home.

But then she'd remember how much visitors always cheered up her mother.

Then again, maybe he'd be in so much pain that they'd have him knocked out.

No, he'd been doing well on the pain medication the hospital had him on. There'd be no reason to go with something stronger.

By the time she pulled into a parking spot, she'd made up her mind. She was just being silly. If there was reason not to visit, she'd simply turn around and go home. No big deal, right?

Mandy checked in at the front desk, smiled at the receptionist who gave her Frank's room number, then started down the hall. There were several elderly residents in the halls. Some acknowledged her with a smile or a nod, but most sat in their wheelchairs, heads down, looking like they were either asleep, or waiting for…

She shuddered. She didn't want to think about that right now.

Room 227. Second door on the right past the nurses' station.

Suddenly, her heart fluttered, and she couldn't catch her breath. The man behind the desk was absolutely gorgeous! Tall, brown hair, brown eyes, broad physique. Oh, my!

Then he looked up and smiled. "Can I help

you?" he asked in a rich baritone.

It was a moment before Mandy could think clearly enough to form the words. "I'm looking for Frank Berglund's room."

"You're almost there. Second door on the right." He pointed, then went back to his work.

And for Mandy, the light suddenly dimmed a little. She allowed herself a small sigh, then continued to the room he'd indicated.

She knocked before she opened the door. Most patients preferred that to someone barging in unannounced. Poking her head inside, she saw him lying in the bed closest to the door, staring up at the ceiling. The bed next to the window was empty.

"Am I disturbing you?" she asked as she stepped inside.

Frank looked over and shook his head. "I'm not exactly busy here."

"I can see that," Mandy said in her best professional voice. "When's your next physical therapy session?"

"Physical therapy?" Frank narrowed his eyes. "In case you hadn't noticed, I have a broken hip. I'm not supposed to be moving around."

"Nonsense!" Mandy exclaimed. "Your hands work fine. Your arms bend. Your head still moves. Your feet and toes still wiggle."

Frank frowned.

"When you are allowed to move that hip, you're going to need all the strength you have to regain what you've lost lying around for so long."

"What if I don't want to? What if I just want to lie here for the rest of my life?"

Mandy pursed her lips. "That's your choice, I suppose. But you're going to have to fight a lot of therapists, nurses, doctors, and me in order to accomplish that."

"Why can't everyone just leave me alone?"

"Do you want a list of reasons?" Mandy asked as she pulled a chair over to sit beside the bed.

"Not really."

"Too bad. You're going to get one," she said. "First, there are people who care about you. People who have jobs to do. People who want to help. And from what I've been told, people you have helped who want to return the favor."

"Big help I am now," Frank huffed. "Not exactly good for anything in this condition. Even worse than I was before."

Mandy shook her head. "I think you need to quit feeling sorry for yourself, Mr. Berglund. There are people in this very facility who have it a lot worse than you."

"And just how am I supposed to help them when I'm stuck flat on my back in this hospital bed?"

He sounded angry now.

Good. There's strength in anger, she thought, then stood up and took a step closer to him.

"That's a very good question. One that will require some thought, creativity, and effort. I suggest you get to it."

"And why would I want to?" Frank asked belligerently. "Why should I?"

Mandy's face softened. "Trust me, Frank. Your life is not over. You have much more to give and a lot to live for. I know this is hard. This is a huge challenge. But you can overcome it and return to the kind of man everyone's been describing to me."

"What have they been saying?" he asked, looking less angry and more bewildered.

"They say you are kind, generous, friendly, a hard-worker, and that you never met a stranger. Just friends you don't know yet. They say you are always the first one there when someone needs help, and the last one to go home when the job is done. I can't imagine that a man so admired would be the kind of man who'd give up so easily."

Frank shook his head. "That man can no longer function. He has MS and a broken hip, remember?"

Mandy sighed. "I remember. But I also think you are stronger than that. Your life isn't over. Just detoured. I'm going to go now and let you think about that."

Without another word, she turned and left the room, passing Mike in the doorway.

Mike watched as she walked down the hall, then shuffled up to the side of Frank's bed.

"I heard that last part," he said. "I know it's none of my business, but I want to add something to her little lecture. A man named Richard Bach said something I'll never forget. 'Here's a test to find whether your mission on earth is finished; if you're alive, it isn't.' Gives ya' something to think about, doesn't it?"

Before Frank could answer, Mike maneuvered his walker back around the bed. He made his way slowly to his side of the room and pulled the curtain between them. His silhouette turned, backed up a few steps, reached down and picked up the power wand for his lift recliner. Frank marveled as the chair's mechanism slowly lowered his roommate to a semi-reclining position. Marvelous invention!

After a few minutes, the only sound in the room was Mike's soft snoring.

Frank listened for a moment and reflected. He was still breathing, so according to Mike's quote, his mission on earth wasn't finished. Something to think about, indeed.

Six weeks later, Frank glared up at his physical therapist.

"Kevin, I hate the water, I told you that!"

"I heard you, Frank," his friend replied. "But the best way to keep your leg muscles functioning is to put you in the aqua-therapy pool. You can work out the other muscles in the gym, but since your legs aren't getting any signals from your brain, they need external stimulus to make them work."

"But…" Frank continued to protest.

"No buts. Doctor's orders."

"I need to have a word with my doctor. Take me to a phone."

"Not until we've finished your therapy, my friend."

As they entered the pool area, Frank noticed a little girl sitting near the edge of the pool. Her tiny body looked frail in her pink butterfly swimming suit, even from the back. Her physical therapist, dressed in matching pink scrubs, was sitting on the edge beside her, talking softly. Even in his belligerent state of mind, Frank couldn't help but see the gentleness in her expression, even as her toned arms rubbed the little girl's back and shoulders.

Kevin wheeled Frank's chair around to the end of the pool, then snapped his fingers. "I forgot my stopwatch. Hang tight, buddy. I'll be right back."

Rolling his eyes, Frank just nodded. A movement caught his eye and he saw the little girl's therapist leave with Kevin, her light brown ponytail dancing as she walked. Puzzled, Frank looked at the girl and gasped. She had no arms or legs! Well, she did have a short stump where her left arm should have been, and a bit longer one instead of a left leg. And she was dangerously close to the pool's edge! What was that therapist thinking leaving her alone like that?

He opened his mouth to say something but closed it when a sweet sound filled the room. He did a double take when he realized she was singing. Her body swayed back and forth in time with the music, each sway bringing her closer and closer to the edge.

"Hey, little girl!" he called. "Be careful!"

Immediately, the music stopped, and she looked over at him, smiling. "Don't worry. I'm always careful. My name's Tawnya, and I'm seven years old. What's your name?"

Grateful that she'd stopped swaying, he answered, "I'm Frank."

"Why are you in that chair?" she asked.

Oh, no. She was going to be one of those kids; the kind who ask a million questions and never shuts up.

"I have multiple sclerosis," he answered shortly.

"What's that?"

Frank groaned inwardly. "It's a disease that makes my brain and my muscles stop talking to each other."

She looked thoughtful for a moment. "So, your brain tells your muscles to move, and they don't?"

"Basically, yeah."

"Bummer. I was born without arms or legs, but it's okay because I have a brain that *can* talk to all my other muscles," she offered brightly.

Frank didn't know what to say to that, so he

settled for a non-committal grunt.

"Do you like to swim?" she questioned.

"Not really."

"Why not?" Her eyes were bright blue and sparkled like she had a secret.

"I've never liked the water."

"Then why are you in here?" her expression was quizzical, like she really wanted to know.

"Because my doctor thinks it will help my muscles get stronger."

"We always have to listen to our doctors, don't we?" she said, nodding sagely.

Frank sighed and looked at the door. Where in the world was Kevin?

"In this case, I'd rather not," he frowned.

Tawnya grinned. "Bet I can make you get in the water."

"What?"

"I said, I bet I can make you get in the water."

"That's probably not a good idea without my therapist," Frank objected.

"Sure it is. The water's not so deep. You could probably touch the bottom easy," she said. "That way you'd be in sooner and finish sooner, right?"

"I don't think it works like…" Frank started. He was interrupted by a loud splash, and suddenly Tawnya was nowhere to be seen.

"Tawnya!" he yelled, searching the water for her. He thought he could see a bit of pink on the bottom of the pool. "Tawnya!"

He leaned as far over as he could, searching

and searching beneath the wave she'd caused. His heart was racing, and his palms were sweaty. Where were those physical therapists? Why weren't they here? They should be saving her!

Finally, when the spot of pink didn't move, Frank's brain turned off, and he reacted without thinking. Wheeling his chair as close to the edge as he dared, he locked his brakes, leaned over, and pushed off with his hands.

The water rushed up faster than he anticipated, filling his nose, mouth, and ears. Instinctively, he flailed with his hands and arms, looking up to the surface of the pool. It seemed to take forever, but in only moments, his face broke the surface, and he was gasping for air, choking on the water remaining in his throat.

With his second gasp of air, he looked down into the choppy water, searching for the tell-tale pink swimming suit on the bottom. When he didn't see it, he took a deep breath and plunged his face back into the pool. Opening his eyes wide, he searched and searched. No pink swimsuit.

I wonder if this pool has a deep end, he thought. *Could she have drifted deeper?* His lungs were burning now, so he lifted his head, again gulping in air. Only this time, he heard something else.

Laughter. A little girl's laughter.

Confusion was followed by anger when he spotted Tawnya bobbing along next to the edge of the pool, her therapist sitting on the edge nearby. Her expression was one of delight and pure joy.

"You did it, Frank!" she chortled. "You got in the pool!"

"You… you…" Frank sputtered. "You little…"

Tawnya just giggled. "I told you I could get you into the water."

"But I thought… You weren't… Why?"

"The doctor said you needed the water to help your legs get strong, right?"

Frank nodded. "Yes, but…"

"You didn't want to get in, right?"

Again, Frank nodded.

"So, I gave you a reason."

Tawnya grinned, and it was such a delightful display of pure pride and joy, that all Frank's anger dissipated. The corners of his mouth turned up a little. She giggled, and his smile broadened. Finally, he couldn't help but laugh with her.

"You win, you little scamp," he admitted. "You got me in the water."

"I sure did!" She looked up at her therapist. "Did you see, Melanie? I got him in the water!"

Melanie nodded and pulled her out of the water, snuggling her tightly in an oversized beach towel. "Ready to call it a day, hon?"

Tawnya nodded, then turned back to Frank. "Have a good swim! Maybe someday, we can race."

With that, Melanie whisked her off, leaving Frank alone in the pool. A moment later, Kevin reappeared.

"Where were you?" Frank asked, his tone reproachful. "A little girl almost drowned while you were gone."

Kevin laughed. "You mean Tawnya? Not likely. That little one is a real fish!"

"But…"

"Congratulations," Kevin interrupted him. "You've accomplished your first task of the day."

"Task?"

"I knew that getting you out of the chair and into the water would be next to impossible. But I figured if I could get your protective instincts to kick in, you'd stop thinking about yourself and your fears. So, I talked to Tawnya and Melanie, and they agreed to help."

"I've been had," Frank stated flatly.

"Yup. Ready to get to work now?" Kevin asked cheerfully.

Frank glanced at the doorway where Tawnya and Melanie had disappeared, then sighed. "Might as well, I'm already wet."

Chapter 9

Frank took a deep breath of the cool morning air. The July sunshine was not as hot as he knew it would be later in the day, and it felt good to be outside. Truth be told, it felt good to be alive. He chuckled to himself as he realized that he wouldn't have said that a month ago.

"Bus is coming," Kevin announced from behind him.

Pulling the brake levers on his wheelchair, Frank shifted in his seat a bit. The bus stopped and they waited while the power the lift creaked its way out of the doorway until the short ramp rested on the sidewalk.

"Just like we practiced, buddy. You got this," Kevin encouraged.

Frank pulled one wheel backward while pushing the other forward, turning one hundred and eighty degrees. He looked over his shoulder to gage the distance, then began backing his wheelchair onto the lift. He was proud that it only took him one try to get nearly centered on the platform. The driver raised the ramp and instructed Frank to hold on.

It always felt a little unsteady when the lift first started rising, but Frank had lost most of his nervousness after the first five times or so. When the lift stopped, he backed into the bus toward the space reserved for wheelchairs. After the driver had his chair strapped down, Kevin took a seat across from him, next to an older man who looked familiar.

"Great job, Frank!" Kevin commended him. "Nary a hitch!"

"Thanks, Kevin," he replied. "I've had a good teacher."

"Frank?" the older man inquired. "Frank Berglund?"

Then Frank heard a soft whimper from under the seat, and it clicked.

"Carl!" he exclaimed. "I haven't seen you in ages! How's Bessie?" He peered under the seat, but the canine face staring out didn't look like the dog he'd nearly tripped over so long ago.

Carl grinned. "Bessie's doing great! She's been paired with a fifteen-year-old girl. I should receive an invitation to their graduation ceremony any day."

"That's wonderful! Who's your new friend?"

"This is Dimples," Carl reached down and stroked the puppy's nose. "This is her first outing since I got her last weekend. She'd rather be jumping up and licking your face than lying under the bench. Today, she's being a good girl," he added as he patted her head.

"She sure is."

Then, Carl eyed him carefully, opened his mouth, then closed it again.

Frank smiled. "It's okay, Carl. You can ask."

Looking relieved, Carl nodded. "Thanks! I hate to intrude, but the last time we ran into each other, you were literally running. What's happened?"

For the next few minutes, Frank filled Carl in on his MS, his physical therapy, and his current focus, navigating his wheelchair in the real world.

He'd just finished his tale when Carl reached up to pull the cord. "This is our stop. It's good to see you, Frank. I wish you continued success!"

"Thanks, it's good to see you, too. I'll probably run into you more often now that I'm mobile. Have a good one!"

Frank watched them depart, smiling as Dimples tried to scamper off the minute her paws touched the ground. Carl had her well in hand, though, and she was soon walking by his side, not perfectly calm by any means, but calmer.

"Friends of yours?" Kevin asked, grinning.

"I'm sorry, Kev!" Frank exclaimed. "That was rude of me! I should have introduced you."

Kevin laughed. "Not a problem, buddy. It's actually a good sign. You're getting more comfortable being on your own. I think when we finish the shopping, I'll let you take the bus back by yourself."

"What? I don't think…"

"I'm sure you're ready, Frank," Kevin interrupted. "You're only picking up a couple of items at the store, so the bag shouldn't be too tricky. I'll be waiting for you when you're finished. And you can always get me on the walkie if you run into a problem."

Frank looked down at the walkie-talkie he wore on his belt. It made him feel a little better knowing he could contact his friend if he got into trouble. "Okay. I'm game."

"Great! Here's our stop."

They quickly found the items Frank needed, and he paid for them, only dropping one quarter in the process.

"All right, my friend," Kevin said. "You're on your own. I'll see you back at Shady Pines."

Taking a deep breath, Frank nodded once, then wheeled off to the bus stop, only a little trepidation in his heart. He only had to wait at the stop for a couple of minutes.

Carefully, he maneuvered onto the lift and into the bus. As he wheeled into the space designated for him, he lost control of the grocery bag in his lap. Scrambling, he nearly fell out of the chair trying to retrieve it from the floor. A delicate hand reached out and picked it up, handing it to him.

Embarrassed, Frank didn't even look at the woman. He mumbled something resembling thank you, then turned his face to the window.

"Excuse me," the woman said. "It's customary to say thank you so the person can actually hear you."

He looked up and saw Mandy grinning back at him.

"I was doing fine," he snapped. "I didn't really need your help."

Mandy's expression fell. "You looked like you could use an extra hand, that's all."

"Well, next time, don't bother."

"What's with the attitude, Frank?" she asked. "I thought we were friends. Just because you dropped a bag is no reason to feel embarrassed. We all drop things from time to time. It's no big deal."

"It's a big deal to me," he mumbled.

"Just who do you think you are?" Mandy sounded angry. "Just because you're in a wheelchair doesn't give you the right to be surly with someone who's just trying to be nice to you. Get a grip, Frank, or you're going to have a very lonely life."

Without another word, she stood and moved to the back of the bus.

The rest of the ride, Frank seethed in his humiliation. How dare she stick her nose in where it didn't belong, then blame him for being mad about it! *She's* the one who was wrong here. She should have minded her own business!

He was so involved in his little pity party that he nearly missed his stop, pulling the cord at the last minute. The bus driver pushed the brakes hard and managed to halt the bus just past the usual stop.

"Next time, give me a little more warning, fella," he said as he unstrapped Frank's wheelchair.

Frank didn't respond as he rolled onto the lift.

Kevin was waiting at the bottom, all smiles. His smile faded as Frank rolled past him without a word.

"What's up, Frank?" he asked. "Did something happen?"

No answer. Frank wheeled in the door, down the hall, and into his room without a word.

Once they were in his room, Kevin closed the door and sat on the edge of the dresser.

"Okay. What happened?"

"Nothing!" Frank growled.

Kevin raised one eyebrow but didn't say anything.

After a few moments, Frank looked up. "Shove off, Kevin. I'm fine. I made it back in one piece, so your job's done."

The physical therapist folded his arms and continued to look at his patient without speaking.

"What? I said you're done. You can go home now." Frank made a big show of putting his bag on the nightstand. He didn't turn around when he was finished, though.

Still, Kevin remained, waiting.

Finally, Frank turned his chair around and sighed. "I've been a jerk, Kev, and I don't know why."

"What happened?"

Frank told him about the interchange with Mandy, and Kevin nodded.

"You're right. You were a jerk."

"I know that!" Frank declared, grimacing. "I just don't know why!"

"If I had to guess, I'd say you were embarrassed, and maybe a little scared. It was your first time on the bus alone. You wanted to prove yourself, and Mandy's gesture of kindness deflated your pride in the attempt."

"So, I was a jerk to her."

"Yup."

"What should I do?" Frank asked, dreading the answer he already knew.

"Apologize. Nicely," Kevin said with a lopsided smile.

Frank groaned. "I was afraid you'd say that. Fine, next time I see her…"

"Not good enough," the physical therapist interrupted. "Now."

"But I don't have her number," Frank tried.

"I do. No excuses." Kevin reached into his back pocket and retrieved his little appointment book.

Frank pulled a pen out of the cup on his nightstand, grabbed a piece of scrap paper and prepared to write. When he had the number down, he reached for the phone, then looked up.

"Hey, how'd you beat me back here, anyway? We left on the bus together."

Kevin looked a little uncomfortable, then hedged, "I borrowed a friend's car and left it at the grocery store."

"You were planning this?"

"Yup. And you did great."

Frank turned back to the phone, paused, then looked at Kevin again.

"It was no coincidence that Mandy was on the bus, was it?"

Ever open and honest, Kevin shook his head. "No. We wanted you to feel as though you were on your own, but also wanted to have a little safety net in place, just in case."

"You tricked me," Frank accused.

"What trick? If you hadn't dropped the bag, you would never have known Mandy was there. For all intents and purposes, you would have been on your own."

Frank shook his head. The logic was sound, but for some reason it irritated him. Still, he couldn't fault them for wanting to make sure he was okay. It just wounded his dignity, again.

I'm really going to have to get over this pride thing, he thought as he lifted the receiver. He reached to dial, then looked back at Kevin.

"A little privacy, please?" he asked, eyebrows raised.

Kevin put his hands up in surrender. "Let me know how it goes."

After he'd gone, Frank started to dial the number. He got five numbers in, then stopped and returned the handset to its cradle. He jumped when Mike spoke.

"Trouble thinking of what to say?"

"Have you been here the whole time?" Frank accused.

"I have," Mike admitted.

"Why didn't you say anything? Let me know you were there?"

"The first rule of roommates is 'Don't interfere with your roommate's affairs'," he replied calmly.

"You could at least have coughed or something, so I'd know you were here."

"Not my fault if you didn't look. I wasn't hiding, just sitting in my usual chair, reading."

Frank didn't have an answer for that, so he just sat.

"Want to practice what you'll say?" Mike offered. "Sometimes that helps."

"Maybe that's not such a bad idea," Frank answered. "What if I start with something like this: Mandy, I'm sorry I was rude to you. It was my first time out on my own…"

"No good," Mike interrupted.

"What? Why not?"

"My wife always said, 'Never ruin an apology with excuses.' It's enough to say you're sorry. You don't have to try and excuse your actions."

Frank thought for a moment. "You mean she doesn't care why?"

"All she wants to hear is that you recognize you were wrong and are sorry for it. Later, after she's forgiven you, she may ask why because she wants to help, but let her ask. Don't offer."

"Interesting," Frank's eyebrows furrowed as he thought about that. "How long were you and your wife married, Mike?"

"Sarah and I were married for sixty-two wonderful years," his roommate beamed proudly.

"And this worked for you?"

"Every time! If I ever tried to make an excuse, she'd plug her ears and tell me she only wanted the apology, not the excuse."

"So, is that your secret to a happy marriage?"

"That, and chocolates. Always bring her chocolates," Mike grinned.

Frank returned his grin and reached for the phone.

Mandy slammed the door as she entered her apartment, seething inside. Her brain told her it wasn't reasonable to be angry with Frank. Logically, she knew where his reactions were coming from. Still, why did he have to be so rude? She'd only been trying to help. It could have been any one of the passengers on the bus who tried to help him. Would he have been as rude to one of them? Probably.

But maybe not. Maybe it was because she was the one who had picked up his bag. He'd been trying out some independence, and she'd interfered when maybe he didn't think he needed help. Maybe she should have waited to see if he could handle it. Or maybe someone else would have offered to help if she hadn't been so quick to jump in.

But he'd been so rude! It rankled, big time!

She marched into the kitchen and pulled open the refrigerator door hard enough that the ketchup bottle fell out. The lid popped open and ketchup squirted a thin line of red on the off-white vinyl flooring.

Ugh!

Grabbing the dishrag from the sink, she attempted to wipe up the mess. But the rag was dry, so she only succeeded in spreading the mess further.

Double ugh!

Just then, the phone rang and there was a knock on her door.

Really? Now?

Glancing at the phone, she decided whoever it was would have to call back. She stood, stepped over the gooey mess, and went to answer the door.

"Hi," Tom said with a charming grin.

"Oh, Tom!" Mandy exclaimed. "I'm so sorry. I forgot we had a date tonight."

Tom clutched at his heart, feigning dismay. "You forgot? Well, that doesn't really bode well for me, does it?" He frowned in an exaggerated display of sadness, then winked at her.

Mandy felt bad. It was their first date, and she wasn't putting her best foot forward. "I'm really sorry. Would you give me a minute? I've got a mess in the kitchen, and I'd like to change out of these scrubs."

"Tell you what, I'll clean up the mess while you change," Tom offered. "That way we can start having fun that much sooner."

"Oh, I can't let…"

"Nonsense!" Tom insisted. "I'm more than happy to help." He glanced around, then headed for the bedroom door. "This way?"

"That way," Mandy said with a laugh, pointing to the doorway on the opposite side of the living room.

"Ah, right." He chuckled and moved swiftly through the doorway she'd indicated.

Mandy listened for a moment, then shook her head and smiled as she heard him whistling. As she walked into the bedroom to change, she marveled. She already felt better, and she hadn't even told him why she'd forgotten their date.

He's a good man, she thought.

Later, as they were enjoying dinner at Lee's Diner, Mandy was impressed with how easily they conversed on a variety of topics. They started with the weather, of course.

"It's sure been hot lately," she began, then made a face. "That's a lame conversation starter, isn't it?"

"Not really," Tom said with a shake of his head. "It's safe and breaks the ice."

"I can buy that," Mandy said, chuckling. "The hot weather makes me think of home."

"Where's home?"

"Florida."

"Ah, hot and humid," he commented.

"Sometimes," she agreed. "The heat here this summer is sure a nice change from the frigid cold I encountered when I moved here, though."

It was Tom's turn to chuckle. "For me, the cold felt like home."

"Where's that?"

"Wisconsin."

"Ooh, brr!" Mandy exclaimed, faking a shiver.

"I'll admit, it can get mighty cold there," Tom said. "I visited Florida once, in August. Between the heat and the humidity, I felt like I was practically melting the whole time I was there."

"That probably wasn't the best time of year to go," Mandy said, looking sympathetic.

"Moving here in March probably wasn't your best plan, either," he replied.

"Hey," Mandy playfully slapped at his arm. "Who knew that winter would be alive and well here in March? I always think of March as the beginning of spring."

"You'd think so, wouldn't you?" Tom

laughed. "So, what do you think of Pine Valley, other than the weather?"

"I like it," she answered. "It's a quaint little place. Certainly different than Daytona Beach!"

"I can imagine! It's different than Madison, too."

"Is that your hometown?" Mandy asked.

"Yup, born and raised," Tom replied.

"Big family?"

"Yup, six siblings," he answered proudly. "What about you?"

"I only have one brother, and he moved away when I was thirteen," she said. "I can't really imagine what a big family would be like."

"It's crazy most of the time, that's for sure!"

"What did you do for fun in Madison?" Mandy asked.

"Skiing," Tom answered without hesitation. "I loved skiing in the Cascade mountains. Of course, they're just bunny hills compared to the Rockies!"

"Bunny hills?" Mandy was confused. She thought they were talking about skiing, not rabbits.

Tom laughed. "That's what we call the little hills where kids learn to ski."

"Oh. That makes sense, I guess. I'll probably need to spend a lot of time on the bunny hill, then."

"You don't ski?"

Now it was Mandy's turn to laugh. "There aren't a lot of snowcapped mountains in Florida."

"I suppose not," Tom replied. "I'd be happy to teach you, if you'd like"

"Really? I'd love that!"

"Great! It's a date. As soon as there's enough snow, we'll go."

"What other date activities do you like?" Mandy asked, truly curious.

"Jazz bands and dancing," Tom replied.

"Me, too!" she exclaimed. "I hear Pine Valley will be hosting a regional jazz festival next year."

"That sounds like fun," Tom agreed. "Will there be dancing, do you think?"

"It's jazz," Mandy responded, "so, I would think so. Are you a good dancer?"

"Oh yeah," Tom said. "You should see my moves!"

Mandy laughed. "I think I'd like that!"

"Good, now we have two dates planned," Tom quipped.

The rest of the meal, their conversation was just as lighthearted and easy. Then, when the waitress brought their ice cream, he innocently asked, "So, how was your day?"

Mandy frowned, then pursed her lips. She'd managed to forget about Frank and his surly attitude. She didn't want to be reminded how rude he'd been, or how angry he had made her feel.

"Not a good time to ask that," she replied curtly.

"Oh, I'm sorry," he responded. "Want to talk about it?"

"Not really."

Tom watched her for a moment, then quipped, "How about them Yankees?"

"What?" Mandy asked, confused.

"The Yankees," Tom repeated. "Do you think they'll win the pennant this year?"

"I don't follow baseball, I'm afraid," she replied, not sure why he was suddenly talking about sports.

"Really? I'm an avid fan," he said.

"Oh?" Mandy asked absently, her mind returning to the Frank situation.

"Oh, yes," Tom continued, seemingly unaware of her inattention. "Whenever my mom would get upset, Dad would start talking about the Yankees."

The incongruity of Tom's statement brought Mandy's attention back to him. "Wait, what? Why would he do that?"

Tom grinned. "Because it worked."

"Worked?"

"Yup," he answered with a nod. "Either Mom would get mad enough at his apparent insensitivity to blurt out what was bothering her, or she'd recognize what he was doing and tell him what was bothering her. Either way, she'd get it out in the open so they could talk about it."

"That's amazing," Mandy said, awe in her voice. "Your father was a very smart man."

"I agree. So, how about them Yankees?"

Mandy couldn't help but laugh. "I don't care

about the Yankees, or any other sports team, Tom. But since you are employing your father's technique, I suppose I should follow your mother's example and tell you about my day."

"Good choice." Tom laughed. "Otherwise, I would have had to start quoting stats and rankings and other such nonsense at you."

"Heaven forbid!" Mandy exclaimed, putting a hand to her forehead in mock frustration. Then, she chuckled, took a sip of her Coke, and sighed. "I had a run-in with Frank today," she began.

Before she knew it, the entire story had tumbled out. Tom listened intently, nodding where appropriate, and making sympathetic noises.

"It's just so irritating!" Mandy finished. "I was only trying to help, and he shut me out completely!"

Tom cocked his head. "Why do you think he did that?"

Mandy glared at him. "Don't go psychoanalyst on me, Tom. I know exactly why he reacted that way. My mom had multiple sclerosis, remember? I've been through all the stages many times with her."

"Okay," Tom nodded. "So, you *know* why, but do you *feel* why?"

"What do you mean?"

"I've found in my nursing work that if I can connect with my patients on a feeling level, it's easier to overlook any rudeness or anger or frustration they may send my way," he replied. "It's not enough to know in my mind what's behind their behavior. For me, I have to try and *feel* what they feel."

"How do you do that?" Mandy was truly curious now. She'd never heard anything like this.

Tom was silent for a moment, then reached over and took her hand. "I know it's our first date, Mandy, but do you trust me enough to do an experiment with me?"

"I think so," she replied, feeling only a little hesitant.

"Good. Come on."

He stood and moved around the table and reached for her hand. She accepted it with a smile.

"Don't worry," he said. "This won't hurt a bit."

She chuckled at the old medical joke and followed him out into the summer heat.

Chapter 10

Frank hung up the phone with a frown. How could he apologize to Mandy if she didn't answer her phone? He glanced over at Mike, who sat in his chair, bearded chin resting on his chest. His book was in his lap, open to the last page he'd read.

Smiling fondly, Frank wheeled quietly out of the room. Might as well let the old codger sleep. Heaven knows he deserved it!

On a whim, he decided to go to the library. Although his double-vision wouldn't let him read anything for very long, he'd recently discovered they had audiobooks. Perhaps they'd have one that would take his mind off the Mandy situation.

As he entered the library, he saw a woman he didn't know sitting next to the window. She was staring out at the flower garden, but he couldn't tell if she was really seeing it or was lost in her own thoughts.

He hesitated, unsure how she'd feel about

being disturbed. He opted for a soft throat-clearing before wheeling further into the room.

She looked over at him and smiled.

"Hello." Her voice was melodic, but a little quavery.

"Hi," Frank replied. "I'm sorry if I'm disturbing you."

"Not at all," she responded. "I was just looking at the flower beds and wondering who takes care of them."

"I think there's a gardener, or groundskeeper, or something," Frank guessed. He really didn't know. He'd never noticed.

"Well," she said, pursing her lips, "They aren't doing a very good job. Those beds need tending. The weeds are beginning to choke out the flowers!"

Frank wheeled to the window and looked out. To his untrained eye, the flower beds looked fine. He glanced at the old woman and decided to keep his opinions to himself.

"I'm Frank," he said, instead. "I don't think we've met."

"I'm Mrs. Hill," she replied, holding out her hand to him.

He took it and was surprised at how frail and thin it was. Still, it matched the rest of her, thin and fragile looking.

"Oh, thank you," she said with a smile.

"For what," Frank asked, perplexed.

"For not squeezing my hand," Mrs. Hill

replied. "I have arthritis, and so many people squeeze and shake so hard that I want to cry by the time they're through."

Frank cocked his head. "Yet, you offered your hand to me," he pointed out.

"Of course, I did," she answered with a huff. "It's the polite thing to do."

"You're right," Frank agreed with a nod. "Have you been living here long?"

"No, I moved in last weekend. My daughter thinks I'm too old to live by myself."

"What do you think?"

Mrs. Hill looked at him with a disgusted expression. "Well, I don't agree, but she didn't give me much choice. She had a buyer all lined up for my house before I'd even packed."

"Ooh, that doesn't seem very nice," Frank commiserated. "I can see why you'd be upset at that."

The older woman looked thoughtful. "Do you know that you're the first person who hasn't taken her side?"

"Really?"

"It's true," she said. "Everyone seems to think it's their job to defend her actions. They say things like, 'I'm sure she had your best interests at heart', or 'There must have been a good reason. Did you fall recently?' "

"Perhaps they were only trying to make you feel better," Frank offered.

"There!" Mrs. Hill exclaimed, pointing a bony

finger at him. "That's the kind of patronizing comment I've come to expect and hate!"

"I'm sorry," Frank hastened to say, realizing she was right. "I wonder if people do that because they're uncomfortable when someone is angry or hurting. I think it's instinct to try and make them feel better so we can feel better. Does that make sense?"

"I suppose," she agreed grudgingly, "but it still makes me mad. It's like my feelings don't matter at all. I'm eighty-seven years old, and I have the right to be angry if the situation calls for it."

"I agree," Frank said. "I need a bit of work in that area. What would you recommend people say to you when you're expressing your anger or frustration?"

Mrs. Hill considered that for a moment. "I think what you said at first was perfect. You said you could understand why I was upset. That made me feel like you really heard me and weren't just patting me on the head. If people really listened and didn't try to fix everything or try to talk me out of what I'm feeling, I think that I'd get over this a lot sooner."

"That makes perfect sense," Frank replied. "Feel free to express whatever you're feeling, and I'll do my best to just listen and not try to fix anything."

Suddenly, Mrs. Hill smiled and reached over to pat his hand. "You're a good boy. Thank you for trying."

Deciding to change the subject, Frank looked at the flowerbeds again. "How do you know so much about flowers?"

"I love flowers, always have," she answered. "My home has eleven flower beds around it. I planted and tended each one myself."

"Eleven?" Frank was shocked. "That's a lot of flowers!"

"It certainly is! There was never a table in my home without fresh-cut flowers all summer long," she announced proudly.

"Amazing! I'll bet they were beautiful!"

"They were. I enjoyed growing, tending, and arranging them," she continued.

Frank thought for a moment. "I wonder if the gardener would object to you helping out a bit."

Mrs. Hill raised one eyebrow. "I thought you weren't going to try and fix anything."

"Right," he acknowledged with chagrin. "I'm sorry."

"That's all right, son," she said with a laugh, patting his hand. "It takes time to change old habits. Tell me about yourself."

"Well," Frank hedged, feeling a little uncomfortable, "I have multiple sclerosis…"

"No, no," Mrs. Hill interrupted. "Tell me about your life before you came here. I want to know about your family, your hobbies, your passions."

Frank realized that this wise woman was the first one here who had asked him that particular question. It was refreshing, but a bit sad to think about his life before MS.

"I'm twenty-seven years old, single, and have worked as a machinist for the past six years," he began. "I have two sisters older than me, and a brother and sister younger. My parents passed away a few years ago, and I don't see my siblings as often as I'd like. They all have busy lives with their spouses and kids."

"Do you miss them?"

"Sometimes," Frank admitted, "but before I was diagnosed, I had a busy life, too."

"What kept you busy, besides work?" she asked.

"Well, in the winter, I went skiing at every possible opportunity. I ran a Christmas tree lot at Christmas time. In the summer, I liked to camp, fish, and hike. Oh, and I love old cars."

"Really? My husband had a 1935 Auburn Speedster in his later years. He loved that car more than me!" she exclaimed, then winked. "Not really, but he did enjoy tinkering with it!"

"I'll bet he did," Frank said with a grin. "I had a 1930 Model A Ford when I was fourteen. I kept harassing my father about getting me a car. He knew I wasn't old enough, but he got tired of me whining about it. So, one day, he took me to a junk yard that a friend of his owned. We wandered around until I saw this Model A and fell in love with it. He bought it for me for $300. We towed it home and parked it in the garage. It never ran, but

I owned a car at fourteen years old!"

Mrs. Hill laughed. "Wise father!"

"Yes, he was. I miss him."

"I bet you do," she replied, patting his hand again. "I miss my Jerry, too."

They were quiet for a few moments, each lost in their own thoughts. Then, Mrs. Hill sighed.

"Well, I think I'll go wash up for supper. Thanks for stopping to talk with me, Frank."

"It was my pleasure, Mrs. Hill," he replied sincerely. "Remember, if you ever need a listening ear, I've promised to try not to fix everything."

"I'll hold you to that, sonny!" she said with a grin. Rising slowly, she picked up the cane that had been hanging on the back of her chair. She looked at Frank and shook her head. "Arthritis in my knees, too, I'm afraid. Don't get old, Frank. It's not worth it."

Chuckling, she walked slowly out of the library, leaving Frank to marvel at her wit and wisdom. Maybe she had a point. Maybe the trouble between he and Mandy was that he wasn't listening. She'd been trying to help him and all he could think about was how embarrassed he was.

Pretty selfish, Berglund, he thought. He pushed the wheels of his chair, determined to do whatever it took to make things right with Mandy.

"Where are we going?" Mandy asked.

"You'll see," Tom replied enigmatically.

After a few minutes of driving in silence, Mandy asked again, "Are you going to tell me what you have in mind?"

"Nope," Tom answered with a grin.

A few more minutes of silence.

"Why not?" Mandy pressed.

Tom laughed. "That would ruin the surprise!"

Mandy tried to scowl but ended up chuckling instead.

After a few more minutes, Tom pulled into the parking lot north of Shady Pines.

"Why..." Mandy started.

Tom pointed a finger at her with a warning look, then touched that same finger to his lips. "Shh," he instructed.

"But..."

"Shh!" he directed more forcefully. "Now, close your eyes. No peeking!"

"Why..."

"Shh! No peeking!"

Feeling a little frustrated and more than a little curious, Mandy did as she'd been told. She closed her eyes and waited. She heard Tom's door open and close, then nothing but quiet. The air in the car began to grow stuffy. Without opening her eyes, she felt for the window crank and turned it twice. A cool breeze wafted in, lightening her growing restlessness. The scent of roses teased her nostrils. She heard crickets and frogs not too far off, singing their evening serenades.

Why had Tom taken her to Shady Pines, and what was he planning?

After what seemed like forever, she heard him returning, but there was another sound in addition to his footsteps. It sounded familiar, but she couldn't place it. She was tempted to peek, but decided the surprise, whatever it was, would be more fun if she played by his rules.

She heard the trunk open, something thudding inside, then it closed. Tom's door opened and she heard him slide in before it closed.

"Did you peek?"

"No, I did not," she replied proudly. "I was tempted, but I resisted."

"Good girl!" He praised. He was silent for a minute then asked, "Wait, are you one of those women who hates being called a 'good girl'?"

Mandy laughed. "Depends on who's saying it and why. Tonight, with you, in this situation, I'll accept it in the spirit it was offered."

"Wonderful."

She could hear Tom's sigh of relief and smiled.

"Can I open my eyes yet?" she asked.

"Not yet. We're going to drive a bit, then the experiment will begin."

"Fair enough," she replied, "but you have to talk to me as we drive. It's bad enough that I can't see where we're going. Silence would be too much to bear."

"Okay," he agreed. "What would you like to talk about?"

"Tell me about your childhood," she suggested. "What was it like having such a large family? Six brothers and sisters, right?"

"Right. I have two older brothers, one older sister, and three younger brothers."

"Only one sister? Did she resent being surrounded by boys?"

"Not that she ever said," Tom replied. "The older boys protected her and us younger boys teased her unmercifully. It was quite the circus at times."

"I can't even imagine," Mandy responded, shaking her head but keeping her eyes closed.

"What about you? What was life like with only one brother?"

Mandy thought about it for a moment, trying to decide how much to tell him. It was their first date, after all.

"I'm not sure how to describe it. It was certainly quieter than what you've described. My brother was just getting to the teasing stage when…" She hesitated, then continued, "when he and my father left."

"Left? I'm so sorry, Mandy," Tom sounded sincere. "I didn't know. We can drop the subject if it's too painful."

"That's okay," she said, realizing that it truly was. "You see, my mother contracted multiple sclerosis and became angry and bitter. After a while, my father couldn't take any more of her negativity. One night, he took Michael and disappeared. We've never heard from him since."

"That's terrible! I don't understand how a man could abandon his family that way!"

"Honestly, I couldn't understand it either, at first."

"What changed your perspective?"

"Living with Mom," Mandy admitted, "taking care of her, listening to her temper tantrums and rantings about how unfair life was, never doing anything well enough to suit her. It was hard to deal with at times."

"Wait, did you say your brother moved away when you were thirteen?"

"That's right."

"Really?" Tom sounded surprised. "That must have been so hard for you! Is that why you went into nursing?"

"Sort of," Mandy replied. "It was actually watching the home health nurse who came in twice a week to help take care of mom. Her name was Mrs. Stailey. She was so gentle and kind, no matter how my mother behaved. After a while, my mother started to mellow out. Mrs. Stailey showed her that there were things she could still do, even on the days when she couldn't get out of bed. She bought yarn and large crochet hooks. Some days, my mom couldn't hold a fork to feed herself, but those hooks were large enough that she could grip them. She started making wooly hats and scarves.

When Mrs. Stailey discovered that Mom loved bright colors, she made sure to bring lots of different colors, along with white and black for accent."

"That was very thoughtful of her!" Tom's compliment warmed Mandy's heart.

"Yes, it was," she agreed. "She turned my mother's life around, and mine. Witnessing what an influence she was for good, I decided I wanted to make that kind of difference in people's lives, too."

"Makes sense. Which leads me to our experiment," Tom said in a mysterious tone as he stopped the car and turned it off.

"Oh?" Now Mandy was truly curious. "How's that?"

"Before you open your eyes, I want you to think about every part of your body and how it works. Your neck, your torso, your back. Every joint from your head to your toes. Keep your eyes closed until I come around and tell you to open them."

"Okay," Mandy agreed, even though Tom's vagueness was truly driving her crazy.

She heard him open his door, get out and shut it again. After a moment, she heard the trunk open, then shut, then her door opened.

"Can I open my eyes now?" she asked.

"Not yet," Tom answered.

She felt him strapping something on her right ankle, then her left.

"What…"

"Okay," he interrupted. "You can open your eyes."

Immediately, she looked down and saw that her ankles were strapped together with a leather strap, the kind they used to secure patients in their wheelchairs.

"What's this?" she asked, not knowing whether to feel angry or annoyed.

"It's part of the experiment," Tom answered, suddenly serious. "You asked how you could *feel* the way your patients feel. We're going to put you through an hour or so of how Frank might be feeling. You can't move your legs. Your arms and hands are fine. Your back is strong. But you don't have use of your legs or feet."

Mandy was still confused. "Why?"

"Because until you can truly put yourself in their shoes, you'll always be subconsciously judging their reactions."

"What will this do?" she asked, pointing to the strap.

"By itself, nothing," Tom admitted. "But when you try to maneuver through some seemingly simple tasks without use of your legs, you'll have a better idea of what Frank and others like him have to deal with. Are you still game?"

After only a moment, Mandy agreed. It should prove interesting, at the very least. She looked beyond Tom to see a wheelchair waiting for her.

"All right," she said with a bit of resignation. "Bring that thing over here and let's get this experiment started."

The next hour was filled with lessons of monumental proportions. Starting with trying to maneuver from the car into the wheelchair. It was harder than she thought it would be, but manageable.

Then, Tom had her wheel herself into the grocery store to buy some oranges. He was insistent on that particular fruit, for some strange reason. The oranges were stacked in a pyramid in the produce section.

Reaching as high as she could, she still couldn't reach the ones on top. So, she tried carefully to remove an orange as close to the top as she could reach, certain that the ones on top of it would come tumbling down. Her worst fears were realized when not only the ones above, but the entire pyramid slid to the floor, oranges rolling every which way.

"Oh, dear!" she exclaimed. "Look what I've done!"

"That's okay, ma'am," a young stock boy reassured her as he knelt down to retrieve the runaway fruit. "I've been telling the boss we shouldn't stack them that way. It's too easy for anybody to knock it over, not just…" he hesitated and looked up at her. "I'm sorry. I didn't mean…"

Mandy waved him off. "Don't apologize. I'm just doing an experiment in what it's like to be in a wheelchair. I'm afraid I'm not starting off very well."

"Well, this wasn't your fault, ma'am," the boy insisted. "I've a mind to go get the manager and show him the results of his 'fancy orange pyramid' display."

Smiling weakly, Mandy said, "Might be a good idea. Do you need me to stay and explain what happened?"

"Nah, I got it covered," he assured her, stood up, and started to walk away. Then, he turned back and asked, "Oh, how many oranges did you want? I can get them for you, if you don't mind that they've been on the floor."

"Um, maybe three?" She looked at Tom, who held up five fingers. "Make that five."

"You bet!" Quickly the stock boy picked up five oranges, put them in a produce bag, and handed them to her. "You have a nice night, now," he said, then walked away.

Mandy looked at Tom. "That was terrible! Can we be done now?"

"Not yet," Tom replied, shaking his head. "This experiment will last a full hour, or we won't find out what we need to know."

"And what do we need to know?" Mandy asked, a bit testily.

"How to *feel* what our patients feel," Tom responded patiently.

Mandy sighed, then pushed the rims of the wheels and moved toward the checkout stands.

"This is your experiment," she called back to him. "Does this mean you're paying for my oranges?"

Tom laughed. "Nope, that would negate one of the steps in this experiment, which would skew the data beyond repair."

"Oh, brother!" Mandy said, rolling her eyes.

As it turned out, checking out wasn't too difficult, although Mandy had a bit of a struggle juggling her purse, the oranges, and her change. Once she was checked out, her purse slung askew on one handle of the wheelchair, and the oranges settled in her lap, she was ready for the next step.

"Now what?" she asked.

"To the bus," Tom directed.

"The bus?" Mandy felt a bit of panic at that announcement.

"The bus," Tom insisted.

"Okay," Mandy said, swallowing her fear and searching for the determination she was sure would get her through this little experiment.

By the time they arrived at the bus stop, Mandy's arms were on fire. It was harder to push the wheelchair from a sitting position than she'd ever imagined. It didn't help that the parking lot ended about a hundred yards from the bus stop. Wheeling over the dirt and rocks was nearly impossible. Tom took pity on her and pushed her the last ten yards or so.

They'd just arrived when the bus pulled up. Mandy had watched patients board the bus several times, so she knew the process. She'd even helped some of them as they backed onto the ramp.

I got this, she told herself.

No, no she didn't. It took her three tries to get her wheelchair lined up enough to roll straight onto the ramp. When the lift began to move, she couldn't help but yelp a little. She looked at Tom, who was standing just in front of her on the ground. She was surprised he wasn't laughing at her. He wasn't even grinning. In fact, he looked concerned.

Once she was inside the bus, it took a bit of maneuvering to back the chair into position so the driver could strap it down. She breathed a sigh of relief when everything was settled, and the bus took off. Only then did she realize that Tom hadn't gotten on with her!

What was he doing? She couldn't do this alone! Where should she get off? How would she get off? How would she get home?

Her mind whirled with fear-filled thoughts and potential scenarios. She couldn't think straight. She couldn't formulate a plan. She felt so anxious that she thought her heart would beat right out of her chest. Her breathing was erratic. Her hands began to shake. She lifted one to her mouth and her bag of oranges slid to the floor. She watched in horror as the oranges rolled around with every turn and jolt of the bus. Tears filled her eyes, and she bit her lip to try and keep some semblance of control.

Suddenly, the bus pulled over and stopped. The door opened and Tom got on. He took one look at her and rushed to her side.

"Oh, Mandy!" he exclaimed. "Are you all right? What's wrong?"

Mandy couldn't speak. She just looked at him, heedless of the tears streaming down her face.

Gently, he stroked her hair, pushing a few stray tendrils back from her wet cheeks.

"It's okay," he soothed. "We'll get you off this thing and back home. You just relax and let me take it from here."

He bent down and removed the strap from her ankles, then looked up.

"Do you want to walk, or shall I push you?"

In answer, she pushed herself to a standing position, willing her shaky legs to hold her up. They did. Holding her head high, working hard to keep her emotions in check, she exited the bus. She could hear Tom folding the wheelchair, but she didn't turn around to watch him carry it off by hand. Once he was off, he unfolded it and jogged to catch up to her, pushing the empty chair.

Thankfully, he didn't say anything. Mandy didn't know whether to be angry or grateful in that moment. All she knew was that she would never forget that experiment. She also felt it would forever change the way she interacted with her patients, especially the ones who took their fear and anger out on her.

Chapter 11

"Mandy! Hey, Mandy!"

Stopping in her tracks, Mandy looked over her shoulder.

"I'm late, Frank," she called back to him. "Can we talk later?"

"This won't take but a minute," he reassured her as he rolled to a stop.

Mandy looked at her watch.

"That's about all the time I have," she said, then smiled to ease the sting of her words.

"I want to apologize for my behavior the other day," he started. "I was way out of line, and I'm sorry. I've been trying to call you, but…"

"Not a problem," Mandy said, waving her hand dismissively. "Already forgotten." She turned to leave, but Frank wasn't finished.

"Did you know there's a Labor Day picnic planned in the park next Monday?" Frank asked. "I think they're planning games with prizes, as well as a full spread of picnic food."

"I think I did hear something about that," Mandy hedged. She knew all about the annual Pine Valley picnic. Tom had just asked her to go with him.

"Well," Frank suddenly looked embarrassed and uncomfortable. "I… uh…"

Mandy looked at her watch again. At this rate, she'd be late reporting for work. Again.

"Spit it out, Frank," she snapped, then sighed. "I'm sorry. It's just that I'm late for work."

"Oh, I didn't mean to make you late," Frank said softly. "I'm sorry. I'll talk with you later, then."

Looking at the disappointment on his face, Mandy felt guilty. Peter would be understanding if she was a few minutes late. He always was.

"That's okay, Frank," she said, trying to sound more cheerful than she felt. "What did you want to talk about?"

"I… uh…"

"You said that," Mandy responded with a grin.

She saw Frank take a deep breath and swallow hard. When he finally spoke, his words were rushed, as though he was afraid he wouldn't be able to get them out if he didn't talk fast.

"I wondered if you'd go with me to the picnic," he blurted.

Now it was Mandy's turn to hesitate.

"Oh, Frank," she breathed. "I'm sorry. I make

it a policy never to date my patients. It creates a weird dynamic that I'm not comfortable with."

Frank's face fell.

"Oh. I didn't think about that," he mumbled.

"I'm flattered that you asked me, though," she said, putting her hand on his shoulder. "Why don't you go to the picnic anyway? I'm sure the whole town will be there, and maybe you'll meet someone who will be perfect for you."

"Yeah, maybe," he muttered.

"I'm really sorry," Mandy tried again, feeling helpless and sad that she'd disappointed him.

Frank was a nice guy, and under normal circumstances, she'd date him in a heartbeat. But these weren't normal circumstances. He was her patient. Besides, Tom had already asked her.

"It's okay," Frank said as he turned and wheeled back down the hallway, passing Tom, who seemed to be in a hurry.

"Glad I caught up to you," Tom huffed as he reached her.

"What's the rush?" Mandy asked.

"You were in such a hurry, you forgot your purse," he said with a grin.

"Oh, man! Where's my head these days?" she asked, accepting the brown bag from him. "That's the third time this week!"

Tom laughed. "Maybe you'd better tie it to your shoulder next time."

"Maybe," Mandy laughed with him.

"I thought you were late for work," he

commented. "Yet, here you stand chit-chatting with Frank. Do I have a reason to be jealous?" He winked.

"No," Mandy said, shaking her head, "but he did ask me to the picnic."

Tom's eyebrows raised. "Oh?"

"I told him I don't date my patients," she said.

"Sounds like a plausible reason," Tom responded.

"I know, but he looked so disappointed. It's got to be tough for a guy in his position to even have courage enough to ask! I felt awful turning him down."

"I can imagine. Still, you are right. It does create a conflict of interest to date your patients. I make it a rule never to date mine for that very reason. I only date cute physicians' assistants," he added with a grin.

Mandy couldn't help but grin. "Like me?"

"Exactly like you!" Tom pulled her into a quick hug. "Now, Mandy, you'd better scoot! You're late!"

"Right! I'm gone!"

Mandy rushed out the door to her car. She knew she'd done the right thing, but it didn't make her feel any better about disappointing one of her favorite patients.

What was he doing here? He didn't really want to be at this stupid picnic. Too many people. Too many activities he couldn't participate in. Too much happiness for the sour mood he was in.

Frank sighed. He knew why he was here. Rachael Bott, the activities director at Shady Pines was quite a persuasive woman.

She should run for office, Frank thought. *I think she could probably sell ice to an Eskimo in winter and sign him up for monthly deliveries in the bargain.*

He looked down at the table where his paper plate was filled with a grilled hamburger and potato salad. It looked all right, he supposed, but he wasn't really hungry. Taking a swig of his water, he put the bottle in the backpack on his wheelchair and looked around for a garbage can. Spotting one at the edge of the pavilion, he put the plate in his lap and began wheeling over.

A movement caught his eye, so he stopped. A bit farther into the park, a woman bent over another garbage can. At first, he thought maybe she'd dropped something in by accident and was trying to retrieve it. Then, he looked closer.

She wore a faded brown sweater over a nondescript cotton dress. The army boots on her feet had definitely seen better days. In fact, when she lifted one foot to delve deeper into the refuse, he saw a large hole in the sole.

Funny, he didn't remember seeing any homeless women in Pine Valley before. Oh, he'd seen a few hobos and vagabonds through the years, but they mostly just passed through during the summer and never stayed too long.

He was about to dismiss the mystery as one not worth spending time on when he noticed Mrs. Whitney, the librarian. She held two plates in her hands with a bottle of water under each arm, and she was making a beeline for the unknown lady hobo.

Frank was intrigued. Did Mrs. Whitney know this woman? Something didn't make sense here, so he continued to watch.

Stopping a few feet away, Mrs. Whitney sat down on the grass and seemed to be speaking to the woman. Frank wished he was a bug on a branch nearby so he could hear what she was saying.

The woman stood up quickly, looked right at the librarian and started to back away.

Mrs. Whitney kept talking and gestured toward the plates of food she'd laid on the grass.

Hesitating, the woman looked back into the trees, then back at the food, then at Mrs. Whitney. Finally, she took one halting step towards the librarian, then another. A few steps later, and she was within arm's reach of the feast.

Frank saw her stop, take a huge breath, and lunge for a plate. Grabbing it up, she turned and raced for the trees, spilling pickles, olives, and potato salad as she went.

Mrs. Whitney shook her head, watching her go. Then, she picked up her own plate of food and both bottles of water. Glancing down at them, she stepped toward a nearby bench and stood the bottles carefully on the arm. With one last glance at the trees, she made her way back to a crowd of people standing near the children's games, munching on a carrot as she went.

What was that all about?

Frank was more than intrigued. Then, he had a crazy idea. Rolling his chair toward the bench, he carefully placed his plate of food next to the water bottles. Maybe the strange woman wouldn't come back. Then, again, maybe she would. Maybe she would appreciate the food he didn't want.

He turned his chair and started to roll back to the pavilion. That's when he saw them.

Mandy and Tom were standing next to the popcorn booth. A girl was handing him a large cup of popcorn. Tom passed it on to Mandy, then turned to pay for it. When his back was turned, Mandy took a handful of popcorn and tossed it at Tom's neck.

Whirling around, Tom grabbed a handful and threw it back at her. They laughed together, then walked side by side toward the carnival rides.

So, that's why Mandy had turned him down! It had nothing to do with him being her patient, and everything to do with wanting to date a man with two good legs!

Frank didn't sleep well that night. Over and over, he saw Mandy and Tom laughing and throwing popcorn at each other. It made his heart hurt. He'd never know that kind of freedom, that kind of fun-filled relationship. He'd lost everything he ever thought was important. Including his ability to give.

The next day, Frank sat alone in the Shady Pines library, feeling sorry for himself. The day after Labor Day was when he used to order the Christmas trees. But there would be no Berglund's Tree Lot this year. No yard full of pines, spruces, and firs. No making deals with the customers. No Cocoa Shack. No marking down of "misshapen" trees. No candy canes for the kids tagging along with their parents.

Instead, he stared out the window, not really seeing the hint of color in the leaves, nor the elementary school children tussling with each other as they made their way home from the first day of school. The sadness that overwhelmed him could not be joked away, could not be ignored, and was becoming a common occurrence in his life.

Why?

He'd asked himself that same question over and over in the past six months. Why MS? Why this damned wheelchair? What good was a man in a wheelchair who couldn't even stand on his own two feet?

As he started to turn away from the window, a movement caught his eye. Kneeling in the flowerbed was Mrs. Hill. After their talk last summer, she'd adopted the flowerbed outside the library window. He marveled that at her age, she still wanted to pull out the last of the summer weeds.

In former years, Frank would have seen her there and would have rushed over to help so she wouldn't have to spend so much time kneeling on her arthritic knees. He knew that if she spent too long in that position, she'd suffer terribly for several days. Now, all he could do was watch and wonder why no one was helping her.

And who was going to help Mrs. Baumgartner shovel her snow this winter? Since her husband had his stroke, Frank had been over after every snowstorm. Now, he couldn't stand up in any weather, let alone when the sidewalk was icy.

What about old Mr. England? That roof of his wouldn't last too much longer. It was as ancient as he was and should have new shingles this fall. Frank had planned to do it, but now… Now, he would be a danger to himself and everyone else around if he tried to climb a ladder.

All his "regulars", those folks who'd come to depend on him for those little and big things they couldn't do themselves, who was going to help them now?

In all his life, Frank had never felt so useless or helpless. It was a horrible feeling, but one that he was afraid he'd have to learn to live with. But how? How does one live a life that feels useless?

Unable to stop the tears, Frank ducked his head and let them fall.

He didn't hear Mike shuffle in. He didn't see

him flop into a chair nearby. He didn't notice the room darkening as the sun set. He was so overcome with his own sadness that nothing else existed.

Suddenly, the lights flipped on, bringing Frank back to present awareness.

"Oh, dear!" the young volunteer exclaimed. "I'm sorry to disturb you. I didn't know anyone was in here. Mrs. Watkins wants the next Lady Pinkerton book, and I said I'd fetch it for her. Do you mind?"

Frank shook his head. "It's okay, Peggy. I'm heading to my room, anyway."

"Mind if I tag along?" Mike said from his chair.

Frank looked at his roommate in amazement, yet again.

"How do you do that?" Frank asked.

"Do what?"

"Sneak up on me so often? The way you shuffle…" he stopped and ducked his head. "I'm sorry. I shouldn't say things like that."

Mike laughed. "Why not? It's true. I do shuffle. If I don't pick up my feet, I'm less likely to lose my balance and fall down."

"But how do you do it so quietly? It seems you're always surprising me."

"Good," Mike stated with a nod. "A little surprise now and again doesn't hurt anyone."

"Well then, lead on, roomie," Frank gestured toward the door. "It's almost time for dinner."

The two shuffled and wheeled down the hall without speaking. When they reached their room, Frank watched as his friend plopped down in the recliner. When he was settled, Mike looked up and cocked his head.

"So, what's got you singing the blues today, buddy?" he asked.

Frank just shook his head. "Nothing worth wasting words on."

"Nonsense!" Mike exclaimed. "Voltaire once said, 'Tears are the silent language of grief'. But Jerry Cantrell said, 'Part of the healing process is sharing with other people who care'. I believe that emotions strong enough to bring tears never heal without words to carry them away from the heart."

Frank just stared.

Mike stared back.

"Two questions," Frank finally broke the silence. "First, how do you remember so many quotes? You have quotes for everything!"

"I find it much more satisfying to read and learn quotes that strike my fancy than to sit and play solitaire all day." He gestured at the deck of cards sitting on Frank's nightstand.

"Hey," Frank protested, "don't criticize my solitaire! My father taught me how to play, and it's comforting to do something with my hands, especially when it reminds me of him."

"That's fair," Mike replied, nodding. "What's your second question?"

"How long had you been sitting there in the

library?"

"Long enough to know you needed a listening ear," Mike said softly.

Frank sighed. "I'm afraid there's nothing you can do about my particular sorrows, my friend."

"You might be surprised. Try me."

Again, Frank was silent, hoping they'd announce dinner so this conversation could end.

They didn't.

Finally, he looked up at the older man. "Have you ever felt so utterly useless that you wondered why you were still taking up space on this planet?"

Mike nodded but didn't elaborate.

Looking down at his hands, Frank looked at the backs, then turned them over and looked at the palms. He held them out for Mike to see.

"These hands," Frank began, "these hands have brought me the greatest joy known to man. The joy of service. I am never happier than when I can help someone. I find more fulfillment in helping an old lady weed her garden than in any job I've ever done. There is more satisfaction in helping a neighbor fix a fence than in creating anything for myself. There is more..." he stopped as the tears threatened to overflow again.

When he'd regained control, he continued, "I sit here in this damned chair and wonder what I am good for now." This time, the emotions took over, and he couldn't contain the tears any longer.

Mike sat silently watching as the torment wracked his friend's mind and soul. When the sobs began to subside, he reached out and patted Frank's hand.

Frank sniffled, then looked up. "I'm sorry, Mike. I can't seem to stop it."

"Don't try," Mike advised. "Tears are there for a reason. I've shed plenty myself over the years. When you're ready, I'd like to give you a little unsolicited advice."

Reaching for a tissue, Frank blew his nose, then took a deep breath. "All right, I'm ready. Advise away."

"You've lost the ability to help people in the ways you've always done. You help them with the physical tasks they can't do for themselves, right?"

Frank nodded.

"Your tears tell me that you haven't lost the desire to help. You still care deeply for the people around you. I'd like to propose that you're not as useless as you think you are."

"But…"

"No 'buts'," Mike interrupted Frank's protest. "We are more than 'the sum of our parts', as Aristotle said. You are not just your physical abilities. You have a heart, a mind, an imagination, and so much more. I invite you to discover those other attributes and put them to work on finding other ways to serve."

Frank frowned. "But without legs to walk, or a back that will hold me up, what can those other things do?"

"You are of the mistaken notion that the only

help you can give is physical labor." Mike smiled. "I'd like to challenge that idea. I'd like you to watch the people around you. See if they serve each other. Observe how they meet each other's needs. I think you'll be surprised."

"All right," Frank agreed. "I'll take your challenge. I'd like to find ways that I can actually be useful again."

Mike grinned. "You're already useful, buddy."

"Oh?"

"Yeah." His grin widened. "I sat down before I refilled my water glass. Would you mind?"

Frank laughed. "I guess I can still reach the faucet, can't I?"

Chapter 12

A couple of days later, Frank and Mike sat together in the common room, which was buzzing with excited residents. Wilson Elementary School was sending over their "Little People Choir". Traditionally, shortly after school started for the year, the kindergarteners would come and entertain.

These children who were just beginning their school experience, and often missing parents and grandparents at home, came with their smiling, sometimes nervous faces, their best clothes, and sweet voices that rarely hit the correct notes. Yet every note was perfect to the residents who looked into their shining eyes, relishing memories of their own school days.

The children filed in, mostly well-behaved. A couple of little boys began tussling over who got to stand in the back next to a particular teacher. Very quickly, the teacher in question took each boy by the hand and stood between them, tall and proud, on the back row.

When the choir was situated, they began to sing under the direction of a teacher sitting in a chair in front of them. Then, Frank did a double take. She wasn't sitting in a regular chair. She was in a wheelchair! Shocked, he realized that he'd been so focused on the children, that he hadn't seen her come in. Amazing!

A shy little boy stepped forward and said in an almost whisper, "We're from Wilson Elementary and are going to sing about animals." Then, he nearly ran back to his place.

The audience chuckled.

Sweet voices opened their little concert with *Froggie Went A'courtin'*. Halfway through the first verse, one little boy, with flippers on his shoes, jumped and hopped to the center of the makeshift stage. A little girl, also with flippers on, hopped to meet him. They hopped back and forth on the stage, getting more and more exuberant as the song proceeded, much to the delight of the residents.

At one point, the boy froggie nearly fell off the front of the stage, eliciting a gasp from the audience. But the girl froggie jumped forward, caught him by the belt, and pulled him back, both landing soundly on their rumps. The boy froggie stood first and helped the girl froggie stand. Everyone clapped and the children beamed.

The concert continued with *The Ants Go*

Marching. Several little "ants" marched forward with pipe-cleaner "feelers" on their heads.

That was followed by *Bingo.* Each time through the song, the children were supposed to clap one letter instead of singing it. One little girl in the middle kept singing and clapping all the way through. Each time she sang while the others clapped, the audience tittered, but she grinned and continued doing it her way.

There's a Hole in the Bottom of the Sea was quite the production. One child placed a black construction paper "hole" on the stage, then retreated as the children sang.

There's a hole in the bottom of the sea
There's a hole in the bottom of the sea
There's a hole, there's a hole,
There's a hole in the bottom of the sea.

On the second verse, a boy dressed as a cardboard "log" stood on the hole, and the children continued.

There's a log in the hole in the bottom of the sea,
There's a log in the hole in the bottom of the sea,
There's a hole, there's a hole,
There's a hole in the bottom of the sea.

As the song progressed, another child came forward dressed in brown. She grabbed the arm of the "log" and then squatted down and ducked her head. Frank was confused. Then the children sang the next verse and he chuckled.

There's a bump on the log in the hole in the bottom of the sea,
There's a bump on the log in log in the hole in the bottom of the sea,
There's a hole, there's a hole,
There's a hole in the bottom of the sea.

At that point, another child dressed as a frog hopped out and the children sang.

There's a frog on the bump on the log
In the hole in the bottom of the sea,
There's a frog on the bump on the log
In the hole in the bottom of the sea,
There's a hole, there's a hole,
There's a hole in the bottom of the sea.

Their song continued as different children emerged dressed as a fly, a wing, and a flea, each one holding onto the arm of the child before and trying to act out their parts. The last verse seemed to bring out the best in them as they sang their little hearts out.

There's a flea on the wing on the fly
On the frog on the bump on the log
In the hole in the bottom of the sea,
There's a flea on the wing on the fly

On the frog on the bump on the log
In the hole in the bottom of the sea,
There's a hole, there's a hole,
There's a hole in the bottom of the sea.

There was a bit of a commotion when the song ended as each child rushed to remove their costumes, then retreated to their places in the choir.

Three little boys came forward then, singing *How Much is that Doggie in the Window*. The choir joined in barking loudly, obviously in competition with each other!

When they started singing *There Was an Old Lady*, Frank grinned. That was a favorite song of his in school. Again, with the production! A little girl dressed in a white wig and apron came out first, obviously playing the old lady. She was accompanied by a boy dressed in black playing the fly.

There was an old lady
Who swallowed a fly
But I don't know why
She swallow the fly
Perhaps she'll die.

Another girl with long, black stockings tied to her waist for legs was the spider. The children sang.

There was an old lady
Who swallow a spider
It wiggled and jiggled
And tickled inside her
She swallowed a spider
To catch the fly
But I don't know why
She swallowed the fly
Perhaps she'll die

Next was a cute little boy with paper wings.

There was an old lady
Who swallowed a bird
Isn't that absurd
To swallow a bird?

The children sang that the bird was supposed to catch the spider who was supposed to catch the fly. Next came a cat, a dog, a goat, and a cow. Each animal was supposed to catch the one before. Finally, out came two children dressed in a horse costume. They nearly tripped over each other as they tried to coordinate their legs. Once they were in position, Frank was ready for the last verse, which he expected to go like this:

There was an old lady who swallowed a horse.
She's dead, of course!

But there, the song differed from the original.

Instead, when they sang, "There was an old lady who swallowed a horse", a precocious little boy loudly accused, "Are you pretending?"

Everyone yelled, "Of course!"

Frank laughed heartily, as did the other residents.

Each song was another lesson in delight for Frank. The children responded warmly to the enthusiastic applause from their mostly elderly audience, who clapped, whistled, and cheered each number.

When the concert was nearly over, several teachers handed out paper autumn leaves to the children, who scrambled down from the stage, singing *It's Autumn Time*. Each little one handed their paper leaf to someone in the audience, then scampered to line up at the door.

Frank grinned at the sweet gesture, enjoying the antics of the kindergarteners lining up.

Then, he felt a tiny hand poke his shoulder.

"Excuse me," a tiny voice said, "would you like a leaf?"

Frank turned and looked down, smiling. Then, tears filled his eyes as he looked into the cherubic face of a blonde-haired, blue-eyed angel balancing expertly on one crutch. Her other crutch was dangling from her arm by a strap as she held out her leaf.

He reached out to accept the gift, almost too touched to speak. After a brief moment, he found his voice.

"What's your name?"

"Grace," she replied, grinning. "What's yours?"

"I'm Frank," he replied, then asked almost reverently. "Grace, did you color this leaf yourself?"

She nodded enthusiastically.

"It's beautiful! Thank you for sharing it with me and thank you for your singing."

"You're welcome!"

"Grace!" a teacher called from the doorway. "Time to go."

"I gotta go now," the youngster said as she turned away. She took two steps, maneuvering the crutches like a pro, then stopped. She looked back, then broke into a huge grin as she turned, took two steps, and made a huge leap.

Unexpectedly, Frank found his arms full of a loving little angel who hugged him with a ferocity he didn't know was possible. He hugged her back, tears flowing freely down his face.

"I love you, Frank!" she whispered.

"I love you, too, Grace," he whispered back.

Then, with a speed he didn't know was possible on crutches, she was gone. In his hand, he held a beautifully scribbled-on leaf with the name Grace carefully drawn on the back. In his heart, he held the memory of undiluted love gifted to him by a five-year-old on crutches.

Frank looked at Mike, who just smiled and nodded.

Chapter 13

Mandy dashed from her car to the front door of Shady Pines. She was late, as usual. She knew Tom would tease her, but he'd understand when she explained about Mrs. Baumgartner's desire to chat. He understood her need to connect with her patients, especially after her experience with their wheelchair experiment. He was great like that.

The late September breeze was a little chilly, so she pulled her sweater tighter as she ran the last few steps to the door. Pulling it open, she nearly ran into Mrs. Hill.

"Good morning, Mrs. Hill," Mandy greeted. "Going to tend your flowers?"

"Not this morning," the older woman replied. "I'm off to the beauty parlor. Time for a wash and set."

"Enjoy that!" Mandy said holding the door open for her.

"Thank you, dear," Mrs. Hill responded, then

shuffled her way outside and down the walk.

Mandy watched her for a moment, then rushed inside to meet Tom for lunch.

Approaching the nurse's station on Wing B, Mandy looked around, but didn't see Tom.

"Hey, Alicia. Any idea where Tom went?" she asked the perky nurse sitting behind the desk.

"I think he's in room 213," she replied. "Probably changing the dressing on Mr. Blake's leg."

"Great, thanks!"

Mandy decided to find her boyfriend rather than waiting at the desk. This time, she could tease him for being late for their date! With a giggle in her heart, she walked quickly down the hall.

"How does that feel, Mr. Blake?" Tom asked just as Mandy knocked on the doorframe. "Oh, Mandy! Is it lunchtime already?"

"It is, and you're late," she said, faking irritation.

"And so are you, if I'm not mistaken," Tom teased back.

"How'd you know?" Mandy asked.

Tom laughed. "Because you're always late."

"I am not!" she protested.

"Yes, you are," Mr. Blake and Tom said in unison.

Mandy's jaw dropped as she feigned offense. Then, she laughed with the two men.

"Okay, you two. You may be right, but do you have to turn it into a chorus?"

"But we sound so good together, don't we Mr. Blake?" Tom asked turning to the older gentleman.

"Like angels in heaven," he replied, then touched Tom's arm. "Ready for the second verse?" he said with a wink.

Tom nodded and, as one, they turned to face Mandy, opened their mouths, and sang an extremely off-key "Ahhhh".

"Make it stop!" Mandy cried, covering her ears and laughing. "I've had enough of your heavenly choir for one day."

On cue, the men stopped and chuckled.

"Until later, then, my friend," Tom said to Mr. Blake. "I'm off to lunch with my girl."

"Enjoy!" Mr. Blake replied and waved at Mandy.

Mandy waved back, then linked her arm with Tom's as they exited the room.

"That was fun," she said.

"Thank you for playing along," Tom replied.

"Well, Tom," she responded, pulling his arm closer. "You're the one who said I should relate to my patients on their level. I'm just practicing what you taught me."

"And doing a find job, I must say," Tom said as he leaned down and kissed her cheek.

"Mmm," Mandy mumbled, "More please."

Tom turned her to face him, then brought his face close to hers.

"You mean more like this?" he asked just

before his lips met hers in a gentle kiss.

Mandy felt herself melt as his arms surrounded her and pulled her closer.

So, this is what love feels like, she thought. *I like it… a lot.*

Breaking the kiss, Tom pulled away a little.

"I only have an hour for lunch, so perhaps we should put this little interlude on hold for the time being?" he suggested.

Mandy sighed. "If we must. Where shall we go?"

As they resumed their walk toward the nurses' station, they didn't see Frank roll his chair backwards into his room. They didn't see the expression on his face, or the way his hands balled into fists, or the tears that threatened to spill out of his eyes.

Frank leaned forward and checked the hallway. No sign of them. Blinking back the tears, he unclenched his fists and rolled out the door and down the hall. Avoiding the apparently happy couple, he headed for the back door and punched the handicap access button hard. The door slowly opened, and he rolled through.

For the longest time, he sat in the back gardens trying to decide if he felt more angry or sad. Something had happened inside him when he saw Mandy and Tom kissing. Like something broke. No, that wasn't right. Like something shattered.

But why would his heart shatter? He wasn't in love with Mandy or anything. He just wanted to date her. She had seemed friendly and… well, safe. She never treated him like an invalid. She treated him like a real person with feelings and desires and abilities.

Yet, she'd turned him down for the Labor Day picnic, and now she was kissing Tom. Maybe she wasn't so safe after all.

Frank suddenly had a great desire to escape this place. Not that he couldn't come and go as he pleased, but he needed a change from his usual routine and the usual people in it.

He remembered there was a small park on the other side of the fence, but it was hidden by the trees. He'd heard about a path that went from the back gardens into the park, but he hadn't found it. On a whim, he decided to look. He was getting better at maneuvering his wheelchair on uneven ground, so he was pretty sure he'd be okay.

It didn't take long to discover the opening, and he was pleasantly surprised to see it had been well-maintained. Enjoying the small thrill of leaving the Shady Pines grounds on his own, he breathed deeply and threw his head back as he rolled along.

Not the smartest move.

His right wheel slipped off the path, and he nearly tipped over!

Better keep your eyes on the road, Berglund, he thought. *That is, if I ever get out of this mess.*

He pushed and pulled at the right wheel, trying to get it back on the path, but to no avail. He thought about trying to stand up and lift it back, but he was afraid he'd end up on the ground, in worse trouble than he was already.

Sighing, he tried again. No luck.

"Need a hand?" a familiar voice asked from behind him.

Frank looked back and then rolled his eyes. "Can't a man enjoy a little freedom on his own, Kevin?"

"Sure, he can," the physical therapist chuckled. "As long as he checks out with the front desk first."

"Ugh!" Frank growled. "Sometimes I feel like a prisoner. Check out with the front desk. Tell them where I'm going and when I'll be back. Check in when I return. I just want to follow this path and see where it leads me. Is that a crime?"

"No," Kevin's expression grew serious. "it's not a crime, Frank, but the rules are there for a reason. What if there was a fire, and we had to evacuate all the residents? What if you were gone but hadn't checked out? Some fireman is going to risk his life running into the burning building looking for you because we think you're still inside. Is that worth your little rebellion against the rules?"

Frank stared at his friend for a long moment,

then shook his head.

"I'm sorry." His voice was genuinely contrite. "I didn't think of it like that."

"I understand." Kevin nodded. "It must be tough to be on your own for so long, then suddenly have to account for your whereabouts every time you leave."

"Yeah. I wish the doc would give me the okay to move into my own place."

"All in good time, my friend. But in the meantime, I want you to think about something. You've been here what… six months?"

Frank nodded.

"Think about Mrs. Sommers," Kevin continued. "She's been living at Shady Pines for nearly twelve years. She has no family left. They've all died. She has no outside friends. They've died, too. The only friends or family she has live right here. You might ask her what it's been like. I guarantee you'll be surprised at her answer."

"I think I'll do that," Frank agreed.

"I'll check you out, but only this time!" Kevin smiled, patting Frank's shoulder. Then he turned back toward the nursing home and disappeared around the corner.

Frank watched where he'd gone for a moment, then looked down. He was still trapped. That blankety-blank man had left without helping him!

Trying to rock the chair back and forth, Frank was determined not to give in to this trap of his own making. He was about to resort to climbing out of the chair to push it out and hope for the best when two boys on roller skates came by. They skidded to a stop and looked him up and down.

"You stuck?" one asked.

"Sure looks like he's stuck," the other one answered.

"Do ya want us to push you out?" the first one queried.

"Well, that depends," Frank answered, looking dubious. "How strong are you?"

"Aw, heck," the second boy said, "Strong doesn't count in this situation. We're smarter than we are strong."

"Speak for yourself!" the first boy exclaimed. "I'm strong *and* smart!"

"Now how is 'smart' going to get me out of this hole?" Frank asked, truly curious.

Both boys grinned, then took off, one yelling, "Hold on! Stay there, and we'll show you!"

Frank couldn't help but laugh at their confidence. Whatever they had in mind, it would surely be entertaining, if not helpful.

In a few moments, they were back, carrying two boards, nearly as long as they were tall.

"What are you going to do with those?" Frank asked.

"You'll see," boy number one said, squatting down beside Frank's stuck right wheel. "Can you roll back just a little?"

Frank pulled on the bar connected to his

wheel, and the chair rocked back a couple of inches.

"Perfect! Now let it roll forward."

He did.

"Now push!" the first boy commanded.

When Frank pushed, he felt the wheel roll onto the end of the board the boy had placed in front of it.

"Hold on!" the second boy called, stepping up to the free end of the first board. He placed the second board just under it.

"Now, roll down here until you're on the second board," he ordered.

Frank wasn't sure what this was accomplishing. It seemed he was just rolling parallel to the path. Surely, they weren't planning to keep placing board after board under his wheel! To what end?

Still, what could it hurt?

So, he pushed, rolling himself until he felt the smaller front wheel drop onto the end of the second board. He kept pushing until the larger back wheel dropped, too.

The boys repeated the process twice more. Then, Frank grinned. Now he saw where they were going with their plan. About twenty feet ahead, the ground rose to meet the path. At that point, he could turn the wheels and regain his traction on the asphalt.

"Wow!" he exclaimed as he continued rolling forward. "That's genius, guys! Thank you!"

"Hurray!" boy one yelled as Frank maneuvered onto the path.

"Yippee!" boy two hollered. "You did it!"

"Oh no," Frank objected. "You two did it! I couldn't even see this rise, and you two found a way to get me here. Incredible! How can I thank you?"

"No need," boy one said as he leaned down to retrieve his skates lying in the grass.

Boy two grabbed his, and they ran off waving behind them. "See ya!" they yelled.

Incredible! Frank thought. *I'll have to find a way to carry boards with me, I guess.* Then, he laughed. As he looked around him, he caught the glitter of water up ahead and decided to explore just a bit further.

The path wound through the trees for a few yards, then wandered down a little incline toward a pond. The scene was so inviting that Frank rolled to the edge without thinking. He sat, enjoying the water, the ducks, and the breeze, which wasn't so cold with the sun on his shoulders.

Giggling children drew his attention across the pond. He saw a young woman with a handful of balloons sitting on a bench. Looking closer, he recognized the homeless woman he'd seen in the park. She wore the same brown sweater over her cotton dress. She was surrounded by several little ones who were laughing at something she said. She joined in their laughter and handed each one a balloon. There was a little dispute over the yellow one, so she held it in the air, high above their heads.

He couldn't hear what she said, but one boy pointed to the little girl he'd been arguing with. The woman smiled, handed the yellow one to the girl, then gave the boy two balloons.

"Woohoo!" he heard as the children scampered away.

One balloon left. A white one. Frank wondered what she would do, since there were no more children in the area.

The woman stood and looked skyward. That's when Frank really looked at her. She had mousy brown hair that matched her shabby sweater. The combat boots looked incongruous with her thin dress. But, he realized, her smile made all that disappear. When she smiled, he couldn't look anywhere else. Her expression embodied joy, and peace, and gratitude all at once.

He wondered what she would do if he called to her. He didn't want her to flee as she had at the picnic.

Without warning, she started singing and let the balloon float as high as it could while she still held on to the end of the string. "Somewhere, over the rainbow, bluebirds fly…"

She continued to sing and watch the balloon bounce on the breeze until the last notes faded. Then, without another sound, she turned, tied the balloon to the bench, and walked briskly down the path away from the water.

Before Frank could shake himself from the magic spell she'd cast, she was gone. He sat for another moment, wondering who might find that white balloon. Would they take it or leave it there?

Suddenly, a gust of wind made him shiver. He turned his chair and wheeled back toward Shady Pines, struggling a bit with the incline he'd rolled down so easily before. But he made it without incident and cheered for his success at the top.

Upon returning to the back gardens, he found Kevin waiting.

"I wondered if you were going to stand me up," he joked.

"Sorry, Kev," Frank replied. "I've just had the most amazing experience!"

"Well, you can tell me all about it while we work," Kevin said as they entered the building together.

Chapter 14

As Frank waited in the checkout line, he recalled how much trouble he'd had the first time he'd returned from a shopping trip on his own. It seemed so long ago, yet barely a month had passed. He'd come so far, but he still hadn't figured out how he could help people the way he used to. It made him sad to think those days were over.

The line moved forward, and he pushed his wheelchair ahead, taking care to stay back far enough to not clip the ankles of the gentleman in front of him with the footrests.

Frank cocked his head to see how many were still in front of him. Oh, good. Almost there. Just then, he noticed a young mother and her three youngsters who'd just stepped up to the register. The little boy couldn't have been more than four years old. He was clutching a Superman pencil box to his chest like it was a life preserver.

The clerk smiled at him and asked if he was buying the pencil box today. He silently nodded and handed it to her. She rang it up, then started to put it in the bag.

The little boy looked shocked and tugged on his mother's skirt. She glanced down, and he pointed to the bag with the box in it. Chuckling, the mother asked the clerk if her son could hold his pencil box.

"No problem," the clerk said, reaching for the box, then handing it to the little boy, who beamed.

The rest of the checkout went smoothly until the total rang up. Frank noticed the mother pale a bit. She counted the money in her hand again, then apologized to the clerk.

"I don't have quite enough, I'm sorry. Can I put a few things back?"

"Of course," the clerk replied, looking sympathetic.

Out of the shopping bags came a small box of cookies, a jar of jam, a bag of coffee beans, and then the mother looked down at her son.

"I'm sorry, Billy," she said, tears filling her eyes. "We can't afford the pencil box this time. Can you please hand it back to the clerk?"

"NO!" Billy cried. "It's *my* pencil box! I *need* it to hold my pencils!"

"I know, son," she said, reaching for the box. "But we just don't have the money right now. Maybe when daddy gets paid again."

"NO! NO!"

Tears spilling onto her cheeks, the mother pulled the box out of his hands and gave it back to the clerk.

"Excuse me, ma'am," the gentleman in front of Frank interrupted gently. "May I help?"

"What?" the mother asked, confused.

"May I help?" he repeated. "May I pay for your extra groceries and the pencil box? I just received a surprise check in the mail, and I'd love to share it with your little family."

"Thank you, but we'll be fine," she protested.

"Nonsense." He smiled. "My grandchildren are too far away for me to spoil. I'd love to give this fine young man the pencil box he obviously loves. And I'm sure your husband will be much more pleasant after his morning coffee."

"Actually, I'm the one who needs the coffee," the mother laughed through her tears.

"All the more reason," he laughed with her. "In fact, I only have a $50 bill, so I'll take care of your groceries this week. I only ask one thing."

"What's that?" she asked.

"That this young man says thank you to the nice clerk."

As the clerk handed the pencil box back to the youngster, he looked at her shyly and said, "Thank you." Then he turned to the man and threw his arms around his knees. "Thank you!"

When the groceries were re-bagged, the mother turned to her benefactor and asked, "How can I ever repay you?"

"Just keep your eyes open," he replied. "If you see someone that could use a little help, and you're in a position to give that help, do it with a smile."

"Oh, I will!" she exclaimed. "May I give you a hug?"

"Of course!" The two hugged for a long moment.

As the mother backed away, she whispered, "Thank you! What's your name? I'd like to remember you in our prayers tonight."

"You can call me Grandpa George."

"I'll never forget your kindness, Grandpa George! God bless you!" Then, she gathered her children and her groceries and left the store.

Grandpa George put his food on the conveyor belt, leaving a bag of coffee, a six-pack of beer, and a pack of cigarettes in the cart. A young man wearing a stockboy's apron walked by, and he called to him.

"Excuse me, young man. I've decided not to buy these after all. Would you mind re-shelving them?"

"Of course, sir," the young man answered, reaching for his cart.

The checkout clerk looked at George in surprise.

"Nasty habits," he chuckled. "I've been meaning to quit, and today seems like a good day to begin."

He paid for his remaining groceries and left the store.

Frank thought about the generosity he'd just witnessed and decided that perhaps he could do without some of the little extras, too. His Tootsie Rolls, for example. Maybe he could cut back on Tootsie Rolls and save that money to help someone else. It wouldn't be much, but maybe it would help someone, sometime. In fact, if he got a job, maybe a seasonal position somewhere, he could squirrel away the money, so he'd have money to share this holiday season!

Great idea, Berglund!

With that, he whistled to himself as he wheeled back to Shady Pines.

Chapter 15

Frank pulled his hat down further over his ears as the late October snow swirled around him. It had been sunny and cold when he left Shady Pines that morning. A perfect day for pumpkin shopping.

He'd found his way to his favorite pumpkin patch, wheeled between the rows of pumpkins, and picked out one that he thought he could manage to take back with him. It wasn't as big as the ones he used to pick out, but it had a couple of little knobs on it that he was sure he could use to his advantage when carving it. A witch with a knobby nose and chin would be fun.

He wheeled toward the bus stop and saw a familiar sight. A thin, older man rode his bicycle on the other side of the road. Frank grinned and waved. Brent smiled and waved back with his usual toothless, happy grin, then ducked his head against the blowing snow.

Brent was nearly a tradition in Pine Valley. He'd been born without soft spots in his skull and hadn't been expected to live more than a few years, since his skull wouldn't expand to fit his growing brain.

Despite the dire predictions, Brent not only lived, but thrived. He was always happy and smiling. He never talked, but that ever-present smile spoke volumes. He rode his bike every day, and always waved cheerily at everyone he saw. He had a cheap little bicycle horn that he used at every intersection.

Frank knew Brent had certain stops he made on his daily route, including the grocery store, a florist, and a bakery. Then, he'd stop at a daycare center where he dropped off the cookies he'd picked up at the grocery store.

His next stop was a nursing home on the other side of town where he delivered a bouquet of white daisies. He'd always put them in a vase on the table in the front lobby where everyone could enjoy them.

His last stop, just before lunch, would be the Senior Citizen Center where he'd deliver day-old rolls and bread from the bakery. The good folks who ran the center would feed him lunch and send him on his way with many hugs and thank yous.

Hm, Frank thought. *Brent finds ways to serve, even in the snow. Why can't I seem to figure this out? It shouldn't be that hard!*

He was so deep in thought that he didn't

notice the tree limb hiding under the snow. Wheeling along, his front wheels hit the limb hard, and before Frank knew it, he was flat on his face in the snow with his wheelchair on top of him.

This feels way too familiar, he thought as he tried to roll over. *Nope, no excruciating pain. That means no broken hip, I hope.*

He gave one huge push, and suddenly the chair was lifted off him. He looked up to see Brent's toothless grin staring at him.

Brent set the chair aside, then held out a hand. Frank took it and pulled as Brent did. But all that happened was he slid on the snow. Frank's back wouldn't support him, and his legs just wouldn't stay put.

"Looks like we're going to need more help, Brent," Frank said sadly. "My back and legs aren't working very well today."

Brent's usual smile turned thoughtful, then he held up his index finger for a moment, his grin back in place. He reached for the wheelchair, pushed it in front of Frank's feet, and put on the brakes. He leaned down and bent Frank's knees, bracing his feet against the front wheels.

"What're you doing, buddy?" Frank asked.

No answer from Brent. He just walked behind Frank and began pushing him to a sitting position. When Frank was sitting up, leaning against Brent's chest, Brent gestured toward the arms of the chair.

"I don't think that's going to work, Brent,"

Frank protested. "If I pull on the chair, it's going to rock forward on top of me."

Silence. Then, Frank felt himself being lowered back to the snow-covered ground. He lifted his head and saw Brent removing his belt and scarf. Now what's he got in mind?

He craned his neck to watch as Brent tied the scarf around one wheel of the chair and a bush on the edge of the sidewalk. He fastened his belt around the other wheel and the fire hydrant on the other side.

"Good thinking!" Frank exclaimed as Brent once again began pushing him from the back.

When Frank could reach the arms of the wheelchair, he grabbed and pulled. He felt Brent's arms underneath his shoulders, lifting him. Brent took several small steps to the side, turning Frank so he was able to sit on the edge of the chair seat. With a bit more tugging and pulling, Frank found himself sitting upright in his wheelchair once again.

"Wow!" he exclaimed. "That was amazing! Thank you, Brent!"

Brent just grinned as he untied his scarf and belt. Then, he picked up the pumpkin out of the gutter and settled it onto Frank's lap.

Just then, Brent looked at the bus stop and started to run, waving his arms as the bus pulled up. He gestured wildly toward Frank. The bus driver gave a thumbs up. Brent returned the gesture and looked back at Frank with the biggest grin Frank had ever seen on that craggy face.

Frank rolled toward the bus as Brent walked to his bike. Just as the lift was rising, Frank waved one last time at his unexpected helper.

Why can't I be more like him? Frank pursed his lips thoughtfully as he watched Brent pedal away.

Chapter 16

"Hi, Cindy. I'm here to apply for the seasonal sales position," Frank announced as he approached the customer service desk at Woolworth's.

The salesgirl peered over the desk at him. "Um, I don't think there's a position open, Mr. Berglund."

"But," Frank frowned, "the newspaper said…"

"Oh, that," she waved her hand dismissively, "I'm pretty sure that position's been filled."

"I see. Well, thank you for your time."

Strange that this girl who'd grown up just down the block from him should dismiss him like some vagabond asking for a handout.

Frank started to turn his chair back the way he'd come in, but stopped when a man's voice asked, "Any applications for that seasonal position, Cindy?"

He heard Cindy hiss as he turned around. The man standing beside her was short and rather dumpy. He had white hair and a bushy mustache.

"So, the position hasn't been filled after all, Mr. Wilson?" Frank asked pointedly.

Cindy had enough conscience to blush as the boss frowned at her before looking at Frank.

"No, Frank," he said, "it has not. Let's step into my office." He looked sheepish as he glanced at the wheelchair. "I'm sorry. Slip of the tongue."

Frank chuckled as he shook his head. "Don't worry about it."

As they entered the small office, John picked up a chair and moved it into the corner. There was barely room for Frank to wheel his chair to a position in front of the desk.

Once he was settled, John slid around to sit opposite him. "Now, Frank, let's talk about what the job requirements are for our seasonal position."

"I'm prepared to do most anything, Mr. Wilson."

Frank felt a bit nervous, although he'd known kindly Mr. Wilson most of his life. Frank could remember coming into Woolworths with his mother when he was just a little tyke. Mr. Wilson always gave him a penny candy as his mother shopped.

"I admire your enthusiasm, son." Mr. Wilson smiled. "If you're hired, you'll be expected to show up on time, work your full shift, and do all tasks assigned to you."

"That's not a problem," Frank answered confidently.

"The tasks you'll be expected to perform would be helping customers as needed, restocking shelves, bringing inventory up from…" he stopped. "I don't mean to be indelicate, Frank, but can you walk at all? There will be a lot of lifting, climbing ladders, and bringing boxes up from the basement."

Frank sat, stunned. He hadn't thought about the physical labor that might be involved in a sales position. He'd envisioned greeting customers, helping them find their purchases, and then ringing them up on the cash register. He was certain he could do all of that. But the ladders, stairs, and boxes of inventory? That was another matter entirely.

"I didn't realize all of that would be required," he said slowly.

"I'm sorry, son," Mr. Wilson said, sounding truly apologetic. "If I could afford it, I'd hire someone to do the inventory and stocking, and give you the sales end of things. I know how personable you are, so that part would be easy for you, but…"

"I understand," Frank said. "If you can't afford two employees, it makes more sense to hire the one who can do the entire job."

"Yes, it does." Mr. Wilson nodded. "I'll keep you in mind if business picks up enough that I need to hire someone else. Would that be all right?"

"Of course. Thank you for your time." Frank had a harder time maneuvering out of the office than he had coming in. But after a few three-point turns, he finally managed to back out.

He wheeled past Cindy at the customer service desk, nodding briefly to her. Once he was out of the store, he stopped and took a deep breath. He'd never been turned down for a job before. It was a very uncomfortable feeling. Downright hurtful! He couldn't fault Mr. Wilson, but still. Would it have cost that much more to hire two part-time employees for the season?

As Frank waited for the bus, his mood slid further and further into the dark abyss he'd felt before. What good was he? He couldn't lift. He couldn't climb ladders. He couldn't manage stairs. He couldn't work. He was a helpless, hopeless, has-been at the ripe old age of twenty-seven… No, twenty-eight. His birthday was next month. Twenty-eight and no prospects.

He sighed as the bus pulled up. No prospects whatsoever.

Frank sat in his room, staring at the playing cards laid on the table in front of him. He hadn't moved a card in nearly twenty minutes. He just stared, feeling those helpless, hopeless emotions he was so familiar with and hated so much.

He looked up when a shadow fell over his cards.

"What's up, Frank?" Mandy asked. "Mind if I take your vitals?"

"Will they let you do that, since you don't work here?" he asked, puzzled.

"I'm filling in for Amy today. Trying to make a little Christmas money, you know."

Frank nodded, "In that case, knock yourself out."

Mandy frowned. "That doesn't sound like your usual chipper self."

"Not feeling so chipper today."

"Oh? Why not?" she asked.

He looked up and shook his head. "It's nothing," he hedged.

Mandy as she wrapped the blood pressure cuff around his arm, pumped it up. She watched the dial, released the pressure in the cuff, and shook her head.

"Not good enough, Mr. Berglund. If it's affecting your blood pressure, which it is, then you need to tell me what's wrong."

"It's really nothing," Frank tried again.

Mandy folded her arms over her chest and stared at him, just waiting.

He tried to wait her out but found himself looking everywhere but at her.

Finally, he focused on her face and glared.

"Fine! I'll tell you." He hesitated for a

moment, trying to decide just how much to tell her. In the end, he decided to tell her everything. He related what happened with the fall in the snow, Brent's cleverness in helping him, and kindness as he waved down the bus for him, and the job he didn't get.

"Were you hurt?" she inquired.

"What?"

"When you fell, were you hurt?" she asked again.

"Just my pride," he replied sullenly.

"Then, what's the problem?" she asked again.

He stared at her for a moment, then all the emotions he'd been feeling since his diagnosis came tumbling out. One event, one incident, one painful reaction at a time.

Mandy listened patiently, and when he'd finished, she nodded her head. "I've heard this before."

Frank scowled.

"Don't get me wrong, Frank. I don't mean to minimize the pain, embarrassment, and helpless feelings you're having. But you are in a much better place physically than you have been since your diagnosis. You're more independent and generally more emotionally stable. But I see you making the same mistakes so many others have made."

"What mistakes?" he asked, feeling angry.

"You have the mistaken notion that because you are in a wheelchair, you can't be useful anymore. I'm here to tell you that you're wrong."

"Just how can I be useful?" he asked petulantly.

Mandy raised an eyebrow. "It won't do any good for me to respond to that, Frank. You need to find that answer for yourself. I suggest you look around you. Watch the people here and see if you can find answers in their day-to-day lives."

Frank sighed. "I believe I've heard that before."

"I'm sure you have," she replied calmly. "There are people here who see your potential and what you are capable of. We all want you to find your new self. The one that finds ways to serve from that chair. I promise, you'll be happier if you do."

"If you say so," Frank sulked.

"Or, you can sit in that damned chair, waste your days playing solitaire, and continue feeling sorry for yourself. Your choice."

With that, she turned on her heel and marched out of the room.

Frank didn't even look up to watch her go. He was seething inside. How dare she! She had no idea what she was talking about.

Did she?

One by one, he recalled Tawnya, then Grace, then Brent, and finally, Grandpa George. Each of them had challenges they faced every day. Yet, somehow, they managed to help and serve those around them.

So, if I want to be like them, and want to make Mandy, Mike, and Kevin proud, then maybe I'd better get these wheels moving and look for more examples, he thought. *Move it, Berglund. As Granny Berglund would say, "Time's a' wastin'!"*

Chapter 17

Frank had his first opportunity as he wheeled down the hall to lunch. Instead of looking straight ahead as he usually did, he moved slowly, glancing into each room. Not so long as to be intrusive, but just a glance to see if anyone was looking out.

Four doors down, he saw a withered little lady lying in her bed, which was situated so she could see out her open door. He caught her grin out of the corner of his eye as he looked quickly away. That grin seemed to be an invitation, so he backed up and looked again. Sure enough, the woman's smile broadened, and she motioned for him to come in.

"Hello," he greeted her.

"Hello yourself," she responded cheerfully. "Come on in and sit a spell. I'm Dorothy, and before you ask, I'm ninety-eight years old."

"I'm Frank, and my mother taught me never to ask a woman's age." He couldn't help but return her infectious smile. "I live four doors down."

"I know." She nodded, and her eyes twinkled.

"You do?"

"Of course. I ask about everyone who passes my door. Even though I can't get out to meet and greet anymore, I like to know who's moved in, and why they're here."

"Really? Why's that?"

"It helps me focus when I'm praying," she said without a hint of embarrassment.

"Praying?"

Now Frank was puzzled. He believed in God, but he couldn't imagine why a perfect stranger would need information about her neighbors in order to focus her prayers.

"Of course!" she exclaimed. "How will I know what to ask for if I don't know why they're here?"

"I'm afraid I don't understand."

"It's not rocket science, sonny." Dorothy chuckled. "I like to spend my alone time praying for specific people and their problems. If I don't know their names or what their problems are, how can I pray for them?"

"Good point," Frank said sincerely. "But who could you ask for such private information?"

"Promise you won't tell?"

Frank leaned in conspiratorially. "I promise."

"I wouldn't want to get anyone in trouble," she admitted. "I usually ask the CNAs, or the housekeepers, and sometimes the nurses, if they're not too busy. The housekeepers are more likely to notice little things, but the CNAs know the more private things. Nobody's supposed to talk about other patients, but they all know why I want to know and are willing to help me. Besides, who am I going to tell besides God?" She laughed at her own joke.

Frank laughed a little with her, but he was impressed by her dedication to the well-being of those around her.

"Dorothy, may I ask why you pray for people you've never met?"

"It's simple." She shifted a little in her bed, then looked up at him. "I used to just say the generic prayers that we all say. The Lord's Prayer, grace on the food, and once in a while, a prayer for something specific. When I could no longer get out of this bed, my prayers became very selfish. I kept praying for a miracle that would allow me to get up and walk again.

"One night, I had a dream. There was a little bear cub lost in the woods. I was hiking and saw it crying next to a huge tree. I didn't want to anger its mother, so I kept walking. But I seemed to be walking in circles, because no matter how far I walked, I kept running across this cub. Still, I was afraid, so I kept walking. Then, I was about to pass the cub yet again when my foot got tangled up in a tree root, and I fell. I tried to stand, but the root held my ankle too tight to yank free. The cub stopped crying and watched me for a minute.

Then, it wandered over and sat down next to me. I kept very still. After a moment, it nuzzled my hand. Gingerly, I reached out to pet its head. I'll never forget its clear sigh of contentment as it nestled down under my arm. As I sat there holding that cub, I worried about its mother, but the warm body next to mine soon had me relaxed.

"Then, I heard a loud crashing sound and was instantly scared again. A large brown bear came barreling through the brush and trees. It stopped by my feet and glared at me. I tried to lay very still, but the little cub nuzzled in closer. The mother cocked her head, looked at her cub, then me, then her cub again. Finally, she stepped up and snuffled her baby. It opened its eyes and yawned, then slipped away from my arms and followed her as she ambled away."

"That's an amazing dream," Frank commented.

"Oh, that's not the end," Dorothy patted his hand. "Listen to this. I was still stuck in the tree root and wondering how I was going to get out. After trying for some time, I laid my head back and looked at the trees above me. There was a beautiful bluebird sitting on a limb just above my head. I watched him for a minute, then he looked straight at me. He started chirping, and it was as if I could understand what he was saying.

" 'Pray for the cub', he said.

"I wasn't sure I'd heard correctly, so I asked, 'What?'

" 'Pray for the bear', it chirped.

" 'Why?' I asked.

" 'Pray for the birds', was its answer.

"I was very confused, but it continued to chirp. Each time, it told me to pray for some other woodland creature.

"Finally, I gave in and prayed for the cub, the mother bear, and every other creature the bluebird had mentioned. The miracle was that when I was finished, I could finally move my ankle again. What's more, it didn't hurt at all."

"Incredible!" Frank exclaimed. "What do you think it meant?"

"Oh, sonny," Dorothy said as she patted his hand again, "I know exactly what it meant. My final task in this life is to pray for everyone and everything I possibly can. So, I keep asking everyone to tell me who needs my prayers. I know that when my last prayer is finished, God will take me into His bosom, and I will once again be able to walk and run and dance like I used to. It's the best and only way I can help others at this point. At least, the ones who don't come to visit me."

"Do you get lonely?" Frank asked, concerned.

"Not too often," she answered, shaking her head, "but it would be nice to get a mortal visitor from time to time. God is wonderful, and His spirit keeps me company always, but... I do so enjoy a good conversation with someone I can touch!" She reached out and patted his hand with a grin.

Frank smiled gently. "I don't blame you there. Perhaps I can visit you from time to time?"

Dorothy's eyes misted over. "That would be wonderful, Frank. Please do."

"I will," he promised.

"Now," she wiped her eyes and her expression turned all business, "who needs my prayers today?"

Frank thought for a moment, then almost shyly responded. "Honestly, Dorothy, I do."

"Tell me about what's troubling you, sonny," she prompted.

For the next hour, Frank told Dorothy about his life before MS, how discouraged and angry he'd become, and how he was on a quest to discover how he could help others despite his disability.

Through it all, Dorothy listened and nodded. When he was finished, she patted his hand once again.

"I don't have a clear answer for you, Frank, except that you're on the right track. I'll pray that God will grace you with an open mind and heart so you can recognize the answers He's going to show you. How will that be?"

"That will be wonderful, thank you!" Without thinking, Frank leaned forward in his chair and as best he could, he put his arms around the frail woman. "Thank you!"

She hugged him back, and when he let her go, he saw tears in her eyes.

"You have given me several great gifts today,

Frank," she whispered.

"What gifts?" he asked.

"The gift of truly listening, the gift of sharing your story, the gift of your touch and your hug. Those are marvelous gifts, and I will treasure them always! Thank you!"

Frank didn't know what to say, so he reached over and patted her hand, tears filling his own eyes. He knew that this encounter was another step in his search for ways to serve.

A few days later, Frank felt anxious and didn't want to stay in his room. The weather was snowy and cold, so he was trapped within the walls of Shady Pines. He wasn't exactly feeling claustrophobic, but he wanted to do something besides play solitaire.

Deciding to find a book in the library, he wheeled himself down the hall, carefully watching the people around him. Everyone seemed to be doing just fine, no need for help from a man in a wheelchair. Still, he smiled and greeted all who paid him any attention at all.

As he entered the library, he took note of several residents who were either perusing the books or sitting in chairs reading. They all seemed content. He sighed, picked a book at random, then wheeled himself toward the windows where the light was better.

But instead of opening the book, he stared out at the snow. It was whirling furiously around the trees and bushes, piling higher and higher on the ground. Frank was reminded of many days he'd spent on the mountain, skiing despite storms such as this. He'd loved to ski, and dearly missed those days on the slopes.

A soft coughing from the doorway caught his attention. He looked over to see Brenda and Kent coming into the room. He'd often seen them together in the dining room but hadn't really paid much attention. Today, he found himself really observing them.

Brenda was a woman in her early fifties, salt-and-pepper hair, with round, pleasant features. She normally walked with confidence and ease, but today, she stepped slowly and carefully.

As he glanced behind her, he saw Kent with his hand on her shoulder. Kent was blind, but always seemed to have a smile on his ruddy face. His eyes were closed, as usual, and he stepped carefully as he followed Brenda.

Frank cocked his head. It wasn't unusual for a blind person to follow with a hand on someone's shoulder, but he knew that normally, they held their guide's elbow. Without conscious thought, he looked down where Brenda's elbow should be.

With a quick intake of breath, he saw she didn't have an arm. In fact, she didn't have any arms! With a stab of shame, he realized he'd never noticed that before. How blind must *he* be!

He watched as they made their way to a table with a newspaper on it and sat down. Brenda quietly described where the paper was to Kent. He reached over and, following her instructions, positioned it so she could see it. Then, she began reading aloud. Kent's smile broadened, obviously enjoying the article.

When that article was finished, Brenda went on to read a couple of headlines. She read one about a local author who was having a new release party in a couple of days.

"Wouldn't it be marvelous to attend?" Brenda sighed. "I haven't been to an author signing since Jean Auel came to town."

"It would be fun," Kent concurred. "I really enjoyed hearing my son read *The Mammoth Hunters*."

"That was a good one," Brenda agreed, "but I liked *Clan of the Cave Bear* better. Many people think her writing got better as she went along, but I liked the rawness of that first book."

"Makes sense," Kent said. "Ready for the next page?"

Brenda said yes, and Kent turned the page. On and on, Brenda read headlines, stopping to read the articles they each wanted to hear. When the last page had been turned, Kent patted her on the shoulder.

"Thank you, Brenda. I do so enjoy hearing the news!"

"And I'm grateful you'll turn the pages so I

can enjoy it, too!" she smiled at him.

Frank watched as the two stood and made their way out of the library.

Hm, he thought, *they each have a disability, but they use what they do have to help each other. So, what do I have? What can I give?*

Feeling even more unsettled, he headed for the dining room to wait for lunch. He turned a corner and saw Mike shuffling in the same direction.

"Hey, roomie!" he called.

Mike stopped and waited for him.

"What's for lunch today?" Frank asked.

"Tuna fish, I think," Mike answered.

"Ugh!" Frank wrinkled his nose. "I think they've served tuna for lunch every day since I've been here!"

Mike laughed. "Not every day, but certainly often enough."

"What say we sneak out and go get a burger?" Frank suggested, only half-teasing.

"A burger sounds good, but I'm afraid my days of walking five miles are long gone, especially in a blizzard."

"It's not five miles to the Burger Barn," Frank protested. "Only… three. And the snow? Just a skiff."

"Still too far and too much snow, my friend," Mike chuckled.

"Fine. I'll suffer with tuna fish, even if it *is* my birthday!"

"What?" Mike stopped and looked at him. "I didn't know it was your birthday! We should have had a party or something."

"Oh, no." Frank raised his hands in defense. "I'm too old for birthday parties."

"You're never too old for birthday parties! Your birth deserves to be celebrated!"

At that moment, the dining room doors opened.

"Surprise!" the crowd inside yelled.

Frank was too stunned to move. A CNA grabbed the handles of his chair and wheeled him inside. The room had been decorated with crepe paper streamers, balloons and a huge sign that read, *"Happy Birthday, Frank!"* There were party hats by each place setting and festive tablecloths on the tables.

"You see, Frank," Mike said, "everyone here knows that each birthday may be their last, so we celebrate each one as if it is. We're glad you moved in here. You've made life a little brighter for each of us."

Frank shook his head. "I haven't…"

"No arguing on your birthday!" Mike scolded. "The rule is that you have to accept every compliment with a thank you and at least pretend you're having a good time. Got it?"

"Got it." Frank grinned.

If these good people had gone to all the trouble to throw him a party, who was he to rain on their parade?

When the party was over, he returned to his room. The discouragement he'd felt before was still there, but these wonderful people had diminished it somehow. He needed to find a way to serve them as much as they served him! Frank Berglund made a birthday vow. He would find a way to serve, no matter what the cost!

Chapter 18

After his visit with Dorothy, Frank decided that attending Sunday services wouldn't be a bad idea. It was getting close to Christmas, and he missed hearing the familiar carols he'd grown up with.

The second Sunday in December, he was sitting in his wheelchair in the back of the meeting room. It seemed to be tradition for all the residents on wheels to sit in the back. He still hadn't figured out why, since there was plenty of room between the rows of folding chairs for wheelchairs to fit. Still, who was he to buck tradition?

This particular afternoon, the usually empty back area was full, so Frank found an empty spot next to the back row of chairs. Adrien, an eighty-two-year-old man who lived on wing C, was already seated in the chair to his left. The visiting pastor began his sermon and Frank settled in to listen.

A few minutes later, Adrien suddenly bent over, nearly hitting his head on the chair in front of him. The man on his other side put his arm around him and bent down to whisper in his ear. Adrien shook his head and slowly sat up, revealing that Mike was the man consoling him.

As Frank looked on, he saw that Adrien had tears rolling down his face, and Mike hadn't removed his arm.

In a few moments, Adrien covered his face with his hands. Mike patted his back as he whispered something. Again, Adrien shook his head and straightened up, staring straight ahead.

The third time, Adrien's frame shuddered as he tried to suppress his grief. This time, he stood up to leave.

Clearly, Frank heard Mike say, "Let me walk with you," as reached for his walker and slowly escorted the distraught man out.

Frank didn't hear the rest of the sermon. He was contemplating the compassion that his roommate had shown. *I have compassion*, he thought, *but I didn't think to put my arm around Adrien or try to comfort him in any way. I could have, but I didn't. Why?*

Unable to find that answer, Frank ducked his head and prayed silently for the answer. If he knew why he didn't act in these circumstances, maybe he could overcome it.

As he returned to his room after the services, he was surprised to see Mike and Adrien sitting together.

"I'm sorry," he mumbled, backing out of the doorway. "I'll come back later."

"No, no," Adrien said as he waved him in. "I'm feeling better now. Please don't let me chase you away."

Frank changed direction and wheeled back into the room. "I'm glad you're feeling better, Adrien. Mike's good for what ails you, isn't he?"

"It wasn't me, this time," his roommate laughed.

"Oh?"

Another neighbor, Ruth, poked her head around the curtain. "I'm afraid I'm to blame," she admitted raising her hand and wiggling her fingers.

Frank rolled closer and saw Ruth sitting on the seat of her walker. Mike was in his usual chair, and Adrien was sitting on the bed.

"What brings you to our bachelor den?" Frank asked, trying to be funny.

"God," Ruth said simply.

Taken aback, Frank didn't know what to say. He just repeated, "God?"

"Yes," the black-wigged woman nodded. "You see, I have a motto. 'If I'm breathing, I'm serving.'"

"That's quite a creed to live by!" Frank exclaimed.

"Yes, but it's kept me sane for many years," Ruth claimed. "You see, about ten years ago, I was diagnosed with Alzheimer's. I was devastated and so frightened! As I felt my memory slipping, I prayed and prayed, promising God everything I could think of if He'd let me keep my sanity or take me to heaven before I lost it completely.

"One night, I was pleading with Him, and I felt a clear answer. It was so simple, really."

"What was the answer?" Frank asked, completely engrossed in her story.

"Serve others," she replied. "I felt strongly that as long as I am alive, I need to be serving somehow. So, every night, I pray and tell God that I've served the best I can and that if it be His will, I'd like to come home now. Every morning, I wake up and realize that there's still someone I need to serve, so I pray and ask who it is. Today, I felt impressed to come to your room, where I found Adrien and Mike."

Adrien took up the story from there. "Today would have been my fiftieth wedding anniversary with my sweet wife. I was remembering her and missing her so much that I just couldn't keep it together. When I realized I needed to leave the services, I intended to go to my room and wallow in my grief. But Mike came with me. He knew that being alone wouldn't help me. I needed to talk. It didn't matter how much I talked, though, I still felt miserable. Then, Ruth came in and set me straight." He chuckled at Ruth's shocked look.

"Set you straight?" Frank asked, looking at Ruth.

"I did no such thing," she protested. "I merely

suggested that he stop thinking about himself and think about others."

Frank nearly groaned. This was sounding too familiar!

"Yup," Adrien interjected. "Ruth reminded me that I had told her some time ago that my wife, Julie, had a gift for making people feel better. She asked me what Julie would say to me if she were here. I had to admit that she'd chide me gently for wallowing too much. Since then, we've been sharing happy memories of our loved ones. It's really helped!"

Frank smiled. "I'm so glad, Adrien! I was pretty concerned when you left the services."

Ruth stood with a bit of effort and smiled at each of the men. "This has been delightful, gentlemen, but my knees are telling me I need to move, or I'll be a permanent fixture in your room.

"May I escort you?" Frank offered without thinking.

"That would be lovely," Ruth replied, beaming. "I haven't been escorted by a handsome gentleman for quite some time."

They wandered slowly down the hall, Frank taking care not to pull ahead as she maneuvered her walker in front of her. There was something on his mind, but he wasn't sure how to approach it.

"Ruth," he began tentatively, "may I ask a question?"

"Certainly!"

"You said you'd been diagnosed with Alzheimer's ten years ago?"

"Yes," she replied, already grinning.

"You seem to…"

"Be just fine?" she finished. "Have it all together? Not struggle with my memory?"

Frank looked sheepish. "You've been asked this before?"

"Many times." Ruth laughed. "I only have a partial answer to your next question, though. Why don't I struggle with my illness? The answer is, I do. Sometimes I can't remember how to put on my shoes and the CNAs have to help me. I can't plan more than an hour or so ahead, or I won't remember what I've planned. I often forget where I am or what day it is. Sometimes, I bump into things because I don't remember they are there, even when I've just looked at them. And please, don't ask me to write anything! I've lost my ability to write even my own name.

"But I think God has given me a gift. He's allowed me to keep enough of my memory to be able to do His work. I often feel who needs to talk, or needs a hug, or who needs someone to serve."

"Wait," Frank interrupted, "someone to serve?"

"Yes, it's just as important to let others serve me as it is for me to serve others."

"That doesn't make sense," Frank protested.

"Sure, it does," Ruth replied patiently. "If no one allowed others to serve them, then who would we serve? If everyone let their pride stand in the way of receiving service, then those who need the blessings from doing service would have no one to help."

Frank frowned as he digested this bit of wisdom.

"Some days, when I wake up, I feel as though someone needs the blessing of helping me somehow. So, I wait until the opportunity presents itself and then allow that service with a smile, making sure to express my gratitude after. That's as great a service as anything I can do for others."

"I never thought of it like that," Frank mused, "but when you put it that way, it makes perfect sense."

"It does, doesn't it? Well, my gallant escort, this is my room. I think I'll take a little snooze before dinner. Thank you for your company!" With that, she leaned in a little and kissed the top of his head. "Remember, service is as much about receiving graciously as it is about unselfishly giving."

As she entered her room and closed the door, Frank watched her, bemused. This little woman had certainly given him a lot to think about today!

A few days after the holidays, Frank woke up to the sound of people hurrying down the hall but trying to appear as though they weren't in a rush to get somewhere. Quickly as he could, he transferred to the wheelchair and pushed himself to the door. Peering down the hall, he saw people coming and going out of Dorothy's room. Not wanting to get in the way, he stayed in the doorway and watched.

"What's going on?" Mike asked.

"Looks like something's happening in Dorothy's room," Frank replied without turning around.

When there was no answer from Mike, Frank glanced back. His roommate was sitting on the side of his bed eyes closed, head bowed. Remembering what Dorothy had told him about her habit of praying for others, Frank bowed his head and offered a simple prayer for her.

Suddenly, the activity down the hall subsided, and Frank knew in his heart that Dorothy had prayed her final prayer.

"God bless you, Dorothy," he whispered, then said a prayer for her family.

He wheeled around and saw Mike watching him, tears flowing down his cheeks.

"She's gone," Frank said.

Mike nodded. "I know."

They spent the next hour talking about Dorothy, and her desire to help no matter what her own situation.

"She was a real example to me," Frank said, "but I want to do more than just pray for people."

"Don't discount prayers, buddy," Mike told

him. "You can certainly do more, but prayer is powerful and helps people even when they don't know you've prayed for them."

Frank pursed his lips, then nodded.

They sat in silence for a few minutes, then Frank looked up. "I need some air. I'll be back in a little while."

"Want some company?" Mike asked.

"Thanks, but I think I need some time alone," Frank answered.

Mike simply nodded and Frank wheeled out into the hall, which seemed unusually quiet for a Wednesday. Without thinking, he stopped in front of Dorothy's door and looked in. The bed was stripped, and a man and woman were gathering her things from the dresser and nightstand.

Suddenly, the woman sat on the bed and buried her face in her hands. The man sat beside her and put his arm around her.

Not wanting to disturb them, he sighed, then rolled on toward the library. As he pushed the door open, he saw a little girl, around eight or nine years old, sitting on the floor in the corner. Her arms were wrapped around her bent legs, her head rested on her knees, and her shoulders shook.

She looked up as he rolled in and hastily wiped her eyes.

"What's wrong?" Frank asked gently.

"Grandmama Dorothy died," she said, dissolving into tears again.

Without thought for his own safety, Frank

leaned forward and rolled out of his chair, catching himself with his arms so his head wouldn't hit the floor. He pulled himself along on the linoleum floor until he reached the girl. Pushing up and twisting until he was leaning against the wall beside her, he put his arm around her.

She leaned against him, clutched his t-shirt with one hand, and buried her face in his shoulder, sobbing.

"I know, I know," he crooned as he wrapped his arms around her. "It's going to be all right. Just let it out."

He didn't know how long he sat there with her, but he heard wheelchairs and walkers passing the library on their way to lunch. Still, they sat together. Then, the same wheelchairs and walkers passed by the other way. Still, they sat. As the afternoon waned on, the light in the library grew dimmer. But still they sat.

Finally, her tears began to subside, and she pulled away, wiping her eyes. Frank dug in his jeans pocket and produced a handkerchief, which she gratefully accepted. He was silent as she dried her tears and blew her nose.

Finally, she looked up at him. "Thank you," she said softly.

"You're welcome. What's your name?"

"Dottie."

"Ah, named after your grandmother, I suppose?"

The little girl nodded. "But she was my great-

great-grandma. She said it was too long to say, though, so I called her Grandmama."

"It's nice to meet you, Dottie. I'm Frank. Your grandmama was my friend, so I don't blame you for crying. She was a very special lady!"

"I know. She always had time to talk to me, even when Mommy and Daddy were too busy. We'd talk about everything; my friends, my teachers, people at church. She wanted to hear everything about my life."

Frank smiled. "Do you know why?"

"She was being nice," Dottie replied. "She was always nice."

"She certainly was! No argument there. But she had a special reason for asking about all those people."

"What was it?"

"She wanted to pray for them," he told her.

Dottie's eyebrows came together in a bewildered frown. "Why would she do that?"

Frank hugged her close to him and taught her what Dorothy had taught him so many months ago. When he was finished, he looked down at Dottie's upturned face.

"So, you see, even when she couldn't get out of bed, your Grandmama Dorothy still helped other people."

"I want to do that, too!" Dottie declared.

"Me, too," Frank agreed.

"Can we pray now?" she asked.

"Of course. That's a great idea! Do you want

to start, or shall I?"

"You first. Then I'll know how."

Silently, Frank prayed for the right words, then he began to pray out loud. "God, we are sad right now because Grandmama Dorothy has died and is on her way to You. Please take her in Your arms and let her know we love her. Help us be more like her every day. Amen."

Dottie repeated the amen, then started her own prayer. "God, I don't know why you needed Grandmama more than me, but she always said you have a plan. So, I'm going to trust your plan and try not to be too sad. God bless Mommy and Daddy, Uncle Ralph and Aunt Susan, Uncle Jim and Aunt Alice. They're going to be very sad like me. But please tell Aunt Beatrice and Aunt Geneva to take good care of Grandmama in heaven. Help me be good and help me remember to pray like Grandmama did. Amen."

Frank squeezed the little girl and said, "Amen."

Just then, the couple Frank had seen in Dorothy's room appeared in the doorway.

"There you are!" the woman exclaimed. "We've been looking for you."

"I'm sorry, Mommy. I was sad and wanted to cry. Nobody was in here, so I came in. This nice man came in and held me while I cried. Then, he told me about how Grandmama wanted to pray for everybody. I want to do that, too!"

The woman leaned down and helped Dottie

to her feet, but the man looked perplexed.

"Pray for everybody?" he asked.

Dottie giggled a little as she reached out her hand to him. "Don't worry, Daddy. I'll teach you."

With a parent on each side, Dottie started to walk away. Suddenly, she whirled back to face Frank, her expression one of horror.

"Frank, can you get back into your wheelchair?"

Her father looked back at Frank, then at the wheelchair. "How…?"

Frank chuckled. "Honestly, I don't know. Dottie needed me, and I needed to be on the floor to comfort her. I'm not sure exactly how that happened."

"Do you need help?"

"Yes, but if you'll tell the CNAs at the desk, they'll send someone. It's kind of tricky to get me back into the chair."

"Are you sure?"

Frank nodded. "Thanks for the offer. And thank you, Dottie, for letting me tell you about my friend."

Dottie broke free from her parents' hands and threw her arms around Frank. "Thanks for getting out of your chair to hold me!"

Frank hugged her tight, then watched her and her parents go. Silently, he said yet another prayer. This one, a prayer of thanksgiving.

"Thank you, God, for Dottie and her namesake, Dorothy. Amen."

Chapter 19

There were red, white, and pink hearts everywhere! Frank couldn't avoid them, and they made him cranky. Valentine's Day! What a crock! He'd never really liked the so-called holiday, but this year seemed especially bad.

Maybe it was because there were visual reminders at every turn. Other years, he'd just avoided going to stores for more than the essentials. His work didn't have hearts everywhere. His house certainly didn't. But here? It seemed that the staff felt it was necessary to remind him that he wasn't married, didn't have a girlfriend, and in his current condition would probably never enjoy those things. It was downright cruel!

He wheeled around a corner and saw a group of residents and CNAs gathered around the nurse's desk. He thought about turning around, going the long way around through the maze of halls and enter his room from the other side. But that thought made him angrier. Why should he put himself out just to avoid the "festivities" of this day?

With a scowl on his face, he pushed himself toward the crowd, aiming for the edge farthest from the nurse's desk.

"Frank!" Mandy called. "Frank, come see!"

Frank sighed. There was no help for it now. He should at least be polite. So, he turned slightly to look at the woman who'd always been there for him.

"What's up, Mandy?" he managed to ask.

She made her way through the crowd until she stood beside him. Holding her left hand out, she gushed, "Isn't it beautiful?"

Looking at her hand, Frank's eyebrows rose. "You're engaged?"

"Yes! Isn't it wonderful?" Mandy almost squealed in delight.

Frank took a deep breath, then let it out slowly as he pretended to admire her ring. "Wonderful," he muttered, then looked up at her. "Who's the lucky guy?"

Mandy looked around, then her smile broadened as she waved to someone Frank couldn't see. A tall, broad-shouldered man with shaggy brown hair made his way toward them. Tom.

"Frank, I'm sure you know Tom," Mandy made the introduction proudly.

"Congratulations," Frank mumbled.

"Thanks!" Tom exclaimed happily, as he put his arm around Mandy's waist.

Frank looked up at him. Then, for some odd reason, he noticed that Tom had hair in his nose. He'd never really noticed that in other people. He wondered if everyone had that or just Mandy's fiancé. He blinked a couple of times as he realized that Tom had asked him a question.

"Pardon? I'm sorry, I was distracted for a moment," he stammered.

"No worries." Tom chuckled. "I just wondered if you were going to the Valentine's dance tonight."

"I don't think so," Frank replied, then tried to soften the admission with a weak smile. "If you'll excuse me, I really need to get to my room."

"Oh, of course," Tom and Mandy said in unison as they stepped aside.

A perfect match, Frank thought. *They're already in sync.*

As he rolled down the hall, he felt worse than before. Alone. Lonely. Hopeless.

A man with no future, he thought, then looked up at the ceiling.

"So, tell me again why I'm here?" he muttered.

The cloud of gloom hung over Frank for the next couple of weeks. Nothing seemed to help. Activities at Shady Pines, trips to the store, rolling through the park on sunny days, playing checkers with Mike; nothing dispelled the awful helpless, hopeless feeling that he was good for nothing and had no future.

"Hey, roomie," Mike said as he touched his hand. "Your turn."

Frank sighed and looked down at the checkerboard. Absently, he picked up a piece and moved it.

Mike chuckled and jumped three of Frank's pieces. "That wasn't the smartest move."

But Frank's mind was already elsewhere, so he didn't even hear his friend.

Cocking his head, Mike waited for a moment, then began putting the game away. He was almost finished when Frank finally noticed.

"Are we done?" Frank asked. "Who won?"

Mike laughed. "I did, by default."

"Default?"

"Yup. You were so distracted, I could have cheated my way to a win, and you would have never noticed. So, I decided that you forfeited the game, which means I won."

"Oh," Frank replied, his thoughts sidetracked again.

After putting the game away, Mike sat back in his chair and watched his roommate with a thoughtful expression.

"What's got you so preoccupied?" he finally asked.

"Hm?" Frank looked up, then shrugged. "Nothing, really."

"I don't believe you," Mike replied. "I haven't

seen you this morose since you first came here."

Frowning, Frank shook his head. "I'm not that bad... am I?"

Mike grinned. "Almost. Spill it. What's eating you?"

Without intending to, Frank did exactly that. He talked about how Valentine's Day made him feel, how Mandy's engagement had only emphasized his feelings of hopelessness, and no matter what he did, he couldn't shake those feelings that he was worthless.

Mike listened intently, nodding occasionally. When Frank finished, Mike leaned forward. "You need a new career, my friend."

"What? A career?" Frank was incredulous. He stared at Mike for a moment, then slapped the arms of his wheelchair. "What kind of career could I do in this thing?"

"There's lots of things you could do," Mike answered calmly. "Office workers sit all day. Why couldn't you do office work?"

"Not smart enough," Frank groused.

"Ah, my friend, 'If you hear a voice within you say, *You cannot paint*, then by all means paint and that voice will be silenced'," Mike quoted.

"Who said that?"

"Vincent Van Gogh," his roommate grinned.

"But he had talent," Frank argued.

"Well, what about a ticket taker at ball games? That doesn't take talent," Mike suggested.

"The only ball games in Pine Valley are little

league and high school. They don't need ticket takers."

"What about taxi driver? Once you were in the car…"

"Double vision, remember?" Frank interrupted.

Mike pursed his lips. "As Henry Ford said, 'Whether you think you can or you think you can't, you're right.' "

"Exactly," Frank frowned.

"What about lion tamer? I'm sure the lions won't mind that you're in a wheelchair, and it would draw huge crowds to the circus, for sure!"

Stunned by the ridiculousness of the suggestion, Frank couldn't say anything. He just stared with his mouth hanging open.

Mike grinned. "Gotcha!"

Slowly, Frank shook his head. Then, a small smile formed, which grew until it was a full grin. Finally, he chuckled. "Only two problems with that."

"Only two?"

"I don't have a lion, and the circus won't be coming to town until August."

Mike snapped his fingers. "Drat! I thought it was a brilliant suggestion!"

Frank threw back his head and laughed. "Oh, it was, my friend. It was!"

After a few moments, Frank looked at Mike. He felt less gloomy, but his problem remained. "Seriously, Mike, what am I going to do with the rest of my life? I don't want to sit around here doing nothing."

Mike grew serious, too. "I don't blame you. You're young and your mind still works. So, let's brainstorm. You were a machinist before this, right?"

"Right."

"What is related to that field that doesn't involve standing, walking, or working directly with the machines?"

"Grinding, bead-blasting, assembling, packing, and shipping," Frank listed, counting on his fingers.

"Are any of those things you could do?"

Frank thought. "Maybe," he answered slowly, "but I can see problems with them. I could grind or bead-blast from my chair, but the maintenance on those machines requires standing, lifting, and bending. I could assemble, but that's going to drive me nuts after a while. Mindless work. Packing and shipping have steps that require lifting heavy boxes."

"Okay," Mike replied. "What else? What about before the machining starts? Are there plans or drawings that machinists use?"

Frank brightened. "Definitely! Engineering the plans, drawing up the plans, checking the tolerances. Lots of prep work before it hits the machine shop." His face fell. "But I don't know much about engineering or drafting. I don't have a degree."

"So, get one," Mike stated matter-of-factly.

"Again, not smart enough," Frank answered, "and no money for school."

Mike leaned back in his chair. "That's fear talking. George Addair said, 'Everything you've ever wanted is on the other side of fear.' I don't buy the 'not smart enough' excuse. As for money, there are grants and scholarships out there. If that fails, there are student loans."

Frank pursed his lips, thinking hard. "I really don't think I have what it takes to be an engineer, but maybe a computer-aided drafter…"

"Now you're talking!"

"I wonder if they teach that at the technical college," Frank mused.

"Only one way to find out," Mike said pointing to the phone. "Call them."

Frank grinned as he reached for the phone book. "No sense waiting, huh?"

"Exactly!" Mike laughed. "Strike while the iron is hot!"

That wasn't so bad, Frank thought as he wheeled through the front doors of Pine Valley Technical College. Then he made a face as he rolled up to the receptionist's desk. He couldn't see over the tall counter surrounding the desk! He stretched as tall as he could, but all he could see was the top of the receptionist's head. Relaxing back, he cleared his throat, hoping to catch her attention.

No response.

He tried again, louder this time.

Still no response.

Frank scanned the top of the counter for a bell. No bell.

Finally, he called, "Excuse me."

The girl stood up and tried to peer over the counter. It was obvious she was too short as she strained to see over the tall barrier from behind her desk. Frank nearly laughed as he watched her bob up and down a bit. She looked like she was jumping. Finally, he heard her mutter something under her breath as she pushed her chair back and came around the barrier.

"I'm sorry," she said apologetically. "I didn't hear you come in, and I can't see over that blasted thing." She gestured toward the ledge and shook her head. "I don't understand why they felt it necessary to wall me off from everyone. I'm supposed to be greeting them, right? It makes no sense!"

Frank laughed. "I agree! Then, when someone comes in who can't stand up next to that wall, how are you supposed to see them?"

"Exactly!" she smiled. "Thanks for understanding. How can I help you?"

"You can direct me to admissions, if you would be so kind."

"Of course. It's just through those doors there." She hesitated. "But you'll have the same trouble in there as you did here. Administration decided we needed to be more 'professional' or some such nonsense, so they installed these 'privacy counters'. I'm sure they are fine for regular people who can stand up to them, but for us vertically challenged individuals and those in wheelchairs, it's just not practical!" She looked around conspiratorially. "But you didn't hear me complain, okay?"

"Maybe you should," Frank suggested. "How will they know there's a problem unless someone says something?"

She looked thoughtful. "Maybe, but I've never been very good at confrontation."

"What if we go complain together?" Frank offered.

"You'd do that?" the receptionist sounded surprised.

"You bet!" Frank exclaimed. "I want to go to school here, but if everything is geared to those of a certain height, it's going to be a problem."

"Good point! Tell you what, let's get you registered first. Then you'll have the added clout of being a registered student. I'll take you in to meet Andrea. She'll take good care of you." She turned toward the doors leading to registration.

"What's your name?" Frank asked as he rolled along behind her. "If I'm going to be raising a ruckus over this, I'd like to know who I'm doing it with."

She laughed. "I'm Pam."

"Hi, Pam. I'm Frank."

"Nice to meet you, Frank."

Pam led the way into the large office where three tall counters shielded the registration desks. She walked around the second counter and spoke to the woman sitting there. In just a moment, both women came back around and smiled at Frank.

"Frank," Pam said, "this is Andrea. She'll get you registered. When you're done, come back and see me. We can then address that 'other matter' we talked about." She winked, then slipped away quietly.

"It's good to have you here, Frank," Andrea said. "Why don't you come around to the side of the desk here? That way we can see each other as we fill out the forms."

As Frank followed her and parked his chair where she indicated, he was grateful she was so friendly; not making a big deal about his wheelchair, but willing to make accommodations for it.

Andrea sat behind the desk and pulled out some forms, placed a pen on top, then slid them across the desk toward him. Before he could even reach for the pen, she put her hand on top of them.

"Before we get into this, I just have to know," she said with a twinkle in her eye. "Just what 'other matter' was Pam referring to? She's not one for secrets, so I'm dying to know what she has up her sleeve."

Frank laughed. "It's my fault, really. We had a bit of a time seeing each other over these high counters, so I talked her into going with me to complain to someone in administration."

Andrea grinned. "Ooh! Can I come, too? I'm not as short as Pam, but these counters make me feel so isolated! When I'm sitting down, I can't see anyone else in the office, and it gets downright lonely. I much preferred the old way where the desks were open to each other with chairs in front of them for people to actually sit down and have a conversation as we are getting them registered. It felt much more friendly and welcoming to me."

"Good points," Frank agreed. "You are more than welcome to tag along. In fact, if any of the other registrars feel the same, they are welcome to come along, too."

"Excellent," Andrea said. "Now, you tackle those forms, and I'll check with the other girls."

"Before you go," Frank interrupted, "I'm going to need help with financing, too."

"No problem," she said. "When you've got those forms filled out, we'll go see David in financial aid. I'm sure he'll have some help for you."

The next couple of hours were a bit of a blur for Frank as he filled out forms, visited a couple of offices in the financial aid department, filled out more forms, and agreed to come back next week after the review committee had decided on what financial aid they could give him.

When he was finished, he wheeled back up to Pam's desk. Rather than wheel up to the front, he slipped around to the side.

"Are you ready for this?" he asked the receptionist.

She looked up from her paperwork and grinned. "I sure am! Andrea asked us to swing through her office first. I don't know what you told her, but there are a couple of the girls who want in on this action."

Frank laughed. "There's strength in numbers, they say. I guess we're going to find out."

As the two of them entered the registration office, they were met by a dozen women and several men.

"What's this?" Frank asked.

Andrea spoke up. "Apparently, we aren't the only ones who aren't happy with the changes!"

"Great! Let's go raise a ruckus!" Frank exclaimed as he started to wheel himself back out the door.

"Um, Frank?" Pam called.

"Yes?" he answered, looking over his shoulder.

"The president's office is this way."

Everyone laughed as Pam led the way down the hall. At the end of the hall, the group stopped, parting the way for Frank to wheel up to the door. He looked up at the sign and suddenly felt intimidated.

Dr. Richard D. Abernathy
President, Pine Valley Technical College

"What's wrong, Frank?" Pam asked. "Go ahead and knock."

"Richard D. Abernathy sounds like a prosecuting attorney's name!" he exclaimed.

Pam cocked her head. "Maybe, but he's just the president of this tiny little school. Nothing to worry about, right?"

Frank nodded his head and grinned. "Aren't I supposed to be supporting you in this little revolution?"

"We're all in it together, Frank," she quipped, and the crowd cheered.

Frank knocked on the door and heard a faint, "Come in."

He turned the knob and pushed, but the door was heavy and started to close before he could get his hand back down to grab the bars on the wheels.

"Here," called a voice from behind him, "let me hold that for you."

A tall, dark man in a faded blue t-shirt and jeans slid up beside Frank. He turned the knob, stepped inside and held the door for everyone to enter.

As Frank passed him, he grinned. "Thanks!"

"No problem," the young man answered.

The elderly man behind the desk looked up and did a double take. "What's all this?" he sputtered.

Without prompting, Pam stepped forward. "Dr. Abernathy, we would like to lodge a complaint."

Frank grinned, silently applauding her courage and audacity.

The president put down his pen, leaned back in his chair, and observed the group. "This sounds serious. Please continue."

Pam began with her meeting with Frank earlier that afternoon. She described, quite eloquently, the challenges she faced as a receptionist who couldn't see those that came in the door.

Andrea stepped forward and talked about her own challenges trying to register students, how it was hard for the students to stand at the counters for so long as they filled out the paperwork and how she had to look up at them, causing neck and eye strain.

Following her, several other registrars shared their own stories about how the tall counters were inconvenient. Then, a couple of the men spoke about other changes that had been made recently that had made their work harder, especially when dealing with students with disabilities. Finally, Pam raised her hand to stop the flow of complaints.

"I think the man who brought this to our attention needs to have the floor." She looked at Frank and gestured for him to speak.

Frank looked around at the group, then at Dr. Abernathy. "Sir, I think these good people have expressed their frustrations very well. My only suggestion is that you listen to those who work with you before making unilateral changes to their work environment. I'm just a potential student here, but the changes they are complaining about are the very ones that will make it more difficult for me to navigate the campus. There may be others that will make the learning environment hard for me. I don't know yet. So, I have a question for you. Are you open to their suggestions? Is your door open for students and faculty to come and express their concerns? Is it your policy to make the school look 'professional' rather than make it functional for all who work and study here? I ask you, sir, what is your response to these good people?"

Dr. Abernathy, who had listened attentively to all who spoke, pursed his lips, tapped his fingers lightly on the arms of his chair, then sat up and leaned his elbows on the desk.

"What's your name, son?" he asked.

"Frank Berglund."

"Well, Frank Berglund, you are a forthright young man. I'm going to keep my eye on you. Not because you're a troublemaker, but because you're going places. You have a keen mind and are obviously a leader. The changes these people have spoken of were made last fall, and this is the first time I've heard of their dissatisfaction. That's because of you, I'm guessing."

Pam nodded. "It is, sir."

Dr. Abernathy smiled at her, then at the rest of them. "I want all of you to know that Mr. Berglund has it right, and I'm sorry I haven't made that clear sooner. My door is always open to students and faculty alike. If you have a problem, a suggestion, or just want to chew the fat, knock on my door. If I'm busy, I'll have you schedule an appointment. If I'm not, let's talk.

"So, here's my answer to your concerns. Let's start by making a list of those things that are detrimental to the performance of your jobs and our students' education. Then, we can make a plan to implement some changes that will work for everyone!"

A loud cheer erupted, and Frank grinned from ear to ear. Dr. Abernathy came around the desk and shook Frank's hand.

"You are going to be a great asset to this school, my boy," he said warmly. "Welcome to PVTC! If there's anything you need or want, you come talk to me, and I'll see that your needs are met."

"Thank you, sir!" Frank replied.

Later, as Frank wheeled back to Shady Pines from the bus stop, he felt such a sense of satisfaction. Not only had he successfully begun the registration process for school, he'd started a positive revolution! Not bad for one day's work!

Chapter 20

Frank sat in the hallway on the first day of class looking up at the students around him. Some were happily chatting in groups, a few were looking at the books in their hands, a couple were looking decidedly uncomfortable.

I don't blame them, he thought. The first day of school can be a bit frightening, especially if you haven't been a student for a while.

His musings were interrupted when a hand was thrust toward him. He looked up to see a beautiful woman with long, fiery red hair grinning down at him.

"Hi, I'm Robyn," she said.

Frank accepted her handshake. "I'm Frank."

"Nice to meet you," she replied formally. Then, she laughed, a deep, throaty, and infectious laugh.

Frank couldn't help but join in.

"Are you in the computer-aided drafting

class?" he asked.

"I am," she replied. "My husband owns a construction company, and we thought it might be helpful if I learned how to draw up plans for him."

"Good thinking," Frank responded.

"What brings you to CAD Drafting?" Robyn asked.

Frank looked down at his chair and decided to play the smart aleck.

"I need to design a new wheelchair, so I thought getting some computer skills would be a good idea."

"Interesting notion," Robyn said, looking thoughtful. "What changes would you make to this design?"

"I was joking," Frank said. "I don't have plans to design wheelchairs. I just wanted to learn something so I can support myself now that I'm in this thing."

"Still, I'm sure the basic wheelchair design hasn't changed much over the years," Robyn observed. "Perhaps it's time to design a new one."

"Well, they offered to get me an electric chair," Frank said, "but I turned them down. It's bad enough that my legs are useless. I don't need my back and arms to atrophy, too."

"Makes sense. So, what bugs you about the chair?" Robyn asked.

Frank thought for a moment. "Well, the rims get cold and wet in the winter. When the ground is uneven or uphill, it's hard to push it. And my hands get so dirty that I hate to touch anything after I've been wheeling for a while."

"There you go," Robyn chortled. "That's the perfect starting point. Maybe that needs to be your final project for this class."

"Maybe so," Frank said with a laugh.

They were silent for a moment, and Frank resumed his observation of the students in the hallway. His eye fell on one woman, and he did a doubletake. She was the woman from the park!

She seemed to be waiting for the classroom to be opened, too, but she wasn't standing with the other students. She had her back against a corner on the other side of the hall, looking studiously down at the load of books in her arms. Her mousy brown hair hung limply around her face. She still wore the shabby sweater, but her cotton dress had been replaced with a clean t-shirt and jeans. Instead of the combat boots, she wore white tennis shoes.

Frank blinked. Yup, the shoes were white, which meant they were new. He wondered what had changed in her life to bring her here with new clothes and shoes. He looked up to try and see her eye color, but she kept her gaze locked on her books.

Turning to Robyn, Frank gestured toward the woman in the corner. She looked where he'd pointed, then nodded and followed as he wheeled over.

As they approached, the woman did lift her

head for a moment. Her expression reminded Frank of a frightened rabbit ready to bolt if anyone moved too quickly.

"Hi, I'm Frank," he introduced himself cheerfully, "and this is Robyn."

The woman looked terrified, but whispered, "I'm Janet."

After that, the conversation got awkward. Robyn and Frank tried to pull Janet out of her timid shell, but she seemed only able to give one-word answers. After a few minutes, the teacher unlocked the classroom, and the crush of students made conversation impossible.

A week later, Frank sighed as he looked at the dismal results of his first math test, then rested his head in his hands. School was turning out to be much harder than he had thought it would be. Too hard! Maybe this hadn't been such a good idea after all.

He sighed again and lifted his head, looking around at the other students working at computers or studying their textbooks. He saw Janet looking down at her book, then up at her computer screen. While she was in study mode, you'd never know she was still quiet, shy, and only a little less terrified.

Frank turned to Robyn sitting next to him on the other side. "I think we need to invite Janet to join us for lunch."

"Good idea," Robyn agreed. "Do you want to ask her, or shall I?"

"I will."

He maneuvered his chair out from under the desk and wheeled down the aisle toward her. Janet glanced up as he approached. She didn't immediately look frightened, which gave Frank a little hope.

"Hi," he began. "Robyn and I were wondering if you'd like to join us for lunch."

She looked down at the small, brown, paper bag sitting next to her backpack. "Thanks, but I brought my lunch."

That was more words than she'd spoken since they'd met!

"Great! You can eat that while we suffer through whatever the cafeteria is offering today."

Janet hesitated, and he thought she was going to refuse.

She took a deep breath and nodded. "Okay."

Frank couldn't help it. He grinned broadly and tapped the back of her chair. "Terrific! I'm looking forward to it."

Feeling better than he had all day, he wheeled back to his desk and gave Robyn a thumbs up. She returned his grin and went back to her studies.

Frank found it difficult to focus, but he did his best to get through his next assignment. Despite his best efforts, he kept glancing back at Janet. Several times, he thought she might be looking sideways at him. She never moved her head, though, so he wasn't quite sure. He noticed that her hair looked fuller, less limp, and definitely cleaner than when he'd first seen her in the park.

Finally, the hands on the classroom clock were sitting on twelve noon. Frank closed his book, tapped Robyn on the arm, and cocked his head toward the door. Surprisingly, Janet met them at the door and actually smiled. Frank was elated!

The cafeteria was busy, as usual. They made their way to a round table in the corner, where Janet took a chair against one wall. She looked overwhelmed and kept her gaze down either at the floor or the table.

Once Robyn was seated, she pulled out her own brown paper bag. Janet glanced up and a tiny smile played across her lips.

"If you'll excuse me, ladies," Frank said tapping the table, "I'll go make my way through the line and get some lunch for myself."

Janet nodded, and Robyn replied, "Don't get lost!"

Frank hurried through the line as quickly as he could, opting for a pre-made sandwich, chips, a brownie, and soda, rather than wait through the longer hot lunch line. When he returned to the table, Robyn was smiling, and Janet looked more relaxed than he'd ever seen her.

"Did you miss me?" he asked.

"Nope," Robyn quipped. "We were having

too much fun getting to know each other."

"Want me to leave?"

"Nah, you can stay," she replied with a grin.

"So, what did you learn about each other?" he asked, hoping to get Janet involved in the conversation.

"I learned that Janet is a whiz at math," Robyn answered.

"Is that true?" Frank looked at the shy woman with hope in his eyes.

She glanced up and nodded.

"Oh, I am envious," he admitted. "I all but failed my first math test today."

"Maybe Janet could tutor you?" Robyn suggested.

Janet looked up, her expression a mixture of shock and horror. "I…" she started, then closed her mouth and looked down at her half-eaten sandwich.

"Would you at least consider it?" Frank asked her gently. "I really could use the help."

Janet looked at him out of the corner of her eye, swallowed hard, then nodded.

"Is that a 'yes' you'll think about it, or a 'yes' you'll do it?" he prodded. When she didn't answer, he slid his brownie toward her. "I'll give you my brownie."

He saw the tiny smile on her lips and knew he'd won. She looked up and nodded. Then, before he could answer, she snatched the brownie and put it in her lap, giving him a brief grin.

He laughed, as did Robyn. After a moment, even Janet snickered a little, although she ducked her head when she did.

The rest of lunch passed quickly, Robyn and Frank doing most of the talking, but Janet added a comment here and there.

One step at a time, Frank thought. *I wonder what kind of woman is hiding under all that timidity and fear.*

Chapter 21

"Aren't weddings supposed to be happy events?" Mike asked, poking Frank's shoulder.

Frank looked at his roommate, then back at his hands clasped in his lap. He shrugged without answering.

"Why so glum?" Mike prodded.

"I'd rather not talk about it right now," Frank answered, gazing out at the couples on the dance floor.

Mandy's wedding certainly hadn't turned out as a happy event for him. The problem was, he couldn't figure out why. He *was* happy for her. She and Tom were well suited for each other. So, what *was* his problem anyway?

His friend watched him for a moment, then pursed his lips. "I think it was Abraham Lincoln who said, 'Better to remain silent and be thought a fool than to speak and to remove all doubt.' Or maybe it was Mark Twain who said it."

Puzzled, Frank looked back at Mike. "First of all, what does that have to do with anything? Second, you truly don't know who said it? I'm shocked!"

Mike laughed. "Actually, it's been attributed to both men, but the original was found in a book by Maurice Switzer called *Mrs. Goose, Her Book*, which was published in 1907."

Holding up a hand to stop him, Frank chuckled. "I didn't mean to start a lecture on the origin of that quote. I was just surprised that you didn't know who said it."

"Ah, but that's the problem," Mike began again. "Since…"

"Uncle!" Frank called, raising both hands in surrender. "I don't care who said it. What does it have to do with anything?"

"You refused to talk about what's bothering you. So, I deduced that you might be afraid that I'd think you foolish for what you're thinking. Instead, you choose to remain silent, which I think is foolish, anyway."

Frank shook his head. "Your logic escapes me, my friend."

"Well, it makes sense to me," Mike argued. "Why don't you tell me what's going on in your head, and we can decide together if it's foolish or not."

Looking up at the ceiling, Frank sighed. "You're not going to let this go, are you?"

"Nope."

"Fine." Frank looked at the bride and groom dancing, staring into each other's eyes like no one else was in the room. "See the happy couple over there?"

Glancing over, Mike nodded. Frank continued.

"I see them dancing. I'll never dance again. I see them so in love. Who's ever going to love me like that? I see them planning a future with kids, a home, careers, vacations… all the things I ever dreamed about. But I don't see those things in my future now. What good is a life without a family of my own? What good am I to anyone?"

Mike raised an eyebrow. "So, it's a pity party, is it? Okay, I'll start the timer now."

"Timer?"

"Right, pity parties are only allowed for ten minutes. Then, it's time to move on to more pleasant topics. Ready, go," he replied, looking at his watch.

"I don't know what you're talking about, Mike," Frank complained.

"Nine minutes."

"I'm not having a pity party," Frank tried again.

"Eight minutes."

"Wait! That wasn't a full minute!"

"Seven minutes."

"I think your watch is running fast," Frank objected, trying to look at Mike's watch.

Mike sheltered his watch against his chest,

raised both eyebrows, and pursed his lips again. "You're wasting time. Six minutes."

Frank threw up his hands in exasperation. "I'm never going to have what I want, Mike, and I don't know how to make myself stop wanting it!"

"What do you want, Frank?" Mike asked softly, lowering his hands back to his lap. "In your heart of hearts, what do you want?"

"I want that!" he exclaimed, gesturing to Mandy and Tom. "I want love, a wife, a family. I want to give and serve and bring joy into this world." He raised a hand to stop Mike from interrupting. "I know, I know. I can serve and bring joy no matter my circumstances, but I still feel incomplete! And only marginally more useful than I was a few months ago. I just don't think I can be happy without a family to care for." He paused, taking a shaky breath. "And I don't know how to fix that."

"Do you know what Charlotte Brontë said?" Mike asked.

Frank rolled his eyes. "No, but I bet you're going to tell me."

Mike shrugged. "Not if you don't want me to." He looked out at the dance floor, a small smile tugging at the corners of his mouth.

Frank sat up and folded his arms across his chest. He refused to give in to this infuriating roommate who seemed to have a quote for everything.

The dance ended and another one began. Still,

the two friends sat in silence. Halfway through the second dance, Frank took a deep breath.

"What did Charlotte Brontë say?"

Mike looked at his friend without turning his head. "Sure you want to know?"

Frank chuckled. "You can be awfully annoying. Did you know that?"

"I know, that's one of my more endearing qualities," Mike said with a chuckle.

"You think so?" Frank asked. "I'll wait to see what your other endearing qualities are before I agree or disagree. What did she say?"

"She said, 'The trouble is not that I am single and likely to stay single, but that I am lonely and likely to stay lonely.'"

Frank frowned. "What are you saying, exactly?"

Mike turned to look Frank in the eye. "I know you want a wife and kids and all that life can give you. Personally, I believe you'll have that when the time is right, but if you sit around moping because you don't have it right now, you'll miss the opportunities life has in store for you in the moment, as a single man.

"You may be single, but you don't have to be lonely. Surround yourself with friends, be social, enjoy music, laughter, and service. Don't give loneliness any opportunity to sneak into your heart. Life is too short to waste it on loneliness and feeling sorry for yourself." He paused. "Okay. You had your ten-minute pity party, and I had my five-minute soap box rant. Let's go have some wedding cake and enjoy this shindig!"

Laughing, Frank agreed. He waited while Mike struggled to stand behind his walker. Sadness flitted across his features as he realized that Mike wasn't as spry as he'd been a few months ago. He hated to think about life without this wise, quote-spewing lifesaver he lived with.

"Coming?" Mike asked over his shoulder.

"Right!" Frank pushed his wheelchair forward to catch up. "Think I could ask for a frosting rose?" he asked.

An hour or so later, the party was winding down. The cake had been cut and eaten, the punch was nearly gone, and only two diehard couples continued to dance to the tired band.

"I think I've had enough partying for one night," Mike said, "and enough wedding cake for several nights!"

"It was good cake, no argument there," Frank agreed. "Want me to go find Rachael and see if our ride is here?"

"Would you? I'd rather not move again until it's time to go."

"Are you okay?" Frank asked.

"Oh, yes. Just too much partying for this old guy. I'll be right as rain tomorrow," Mike reassured him.

"Okay. I'll be right back."

Frank wheeled away in search of the Shady Pines activity director, Rachael Bott. She'd been so good to make sure everyone who wanted to attend had transportation to the reception.

"Frank!" a familiar voice called.

He turned around to see Mandy running toward him across the dance floor. She'd changed out of her wedding gown into a sleek, peach-colored suit.

Frank whistled and affected his best fashion critic voice. "I thought you looked amazing in your wedding gown, Mandy, but that color is fabulous on you!"

Mandy laughed. "I'm glad I caught you! I wanted to thank you for coming. I know how hard it can be to get out sometimes."

"You'll have to thank Rachael for that one," he replied. "Without her, I'd still be wheeling over from Shady Pines."

"That's what I mean," Mandy said. "You would have come no matter what. That means a lot to me. I want you to know that just because I'm married doesn't mean we can't be friends. If you ever need anything…"

"I know," Frank interrupted, "call you."

Mandy put her hand on his arm. "I'm serious. MS can be a roller coaster of emotions, even after you've had it for years. I'm here if you ever need a sounding board."

Frank looked in her eyes and was touched by the sincerity he saw there. "Thanks, Mandy. I'll remember that. Now, don't you have a husband waiting to take you on a honeymoon?"

He winked and looked over her shoulder at Tom, who had followed her with an understanding smile.

"I know we don't know each other very well, Frank," the groom said, stepping forward, "I haven't had the opportunity to work on your ward very often, but any friend of Mandy's is a friend of mine. Our door is always open to you."

"Thanks, Tom. That's really nice of you." Frank cleared his throat. "Enough procrastinating, you two! Go get your honeymoon started already!"

The happy couple laughed, joined hands, and ran for the outside door, waving as they disappeared through it.

Frank watched them go and thought about Mike's advice. Taking a deep breath, he nodded. He could do this. He *would* do this! From this moment on, loneliness wouldn't exist for him. He simply wouldn't allow it!

Chapter 22

The next morning, Frank woke and stretched. Glancing at the curtain dividing his bed from Mike's, he was surprised it was still pulled shut. Mike didn't usually sleep late.

"Good morning, sleepy-head," he called.

No answer.

Frank frowned.

"Mike? You awake?"

Silence.

Becoming concerned, Frank pushed his legs off the edge of the bed and sat up. Transferring to his wheelchair, he pushed himself over to the curtain and peered around it.

"Mike?"

No response.

Truly alarmed now, Frank pushed the curtain aside and wheeled to the side of the bed. He peered down into his friend's ashen face. Shaking Mike's shoulder, he called again.

"Mike! Wake up, buddy! You're scaring me!"

Still no reply, but Frank saw Mike's right finger twitch.

"Okay, good. You're still alive. I'm going to call the nurse." He pushed the call button on the side rail, then took Mike's hand in his. "Hang on, Mike. Help is on the way."

Two minutes later, the nurse came in, took one look at Mike's face, and picked up the phone to dial 911. While they waited for the ambulance, she checked his pulse, his pupil reaction, and blood pressure. By the time she'd finished her assessment, the paramedics had arrived.

Frank backed out of the way to let them do their work, praying all the while that his friend would pull through.

After they'd lifted Mike onto the gurney and wheeled him out, Frank sat alone, feeling scared and worried. What if his roommate didn't make it? What if he lost the best friend, and best advisor, he'd ever had?

Suddenly, the room seemed too big and too empty. Frank turned his wheelchair toward the door and pushed hard. He nearly ran into a group of residents heading for the dining room. Mindlessly, he followed behind them.

The door to the dining room opened and Frank was assaulted by the sights, sounds, and smells of breakfast being served to hungry, mostly happy residents. It was too much!

He backed away and headed for the library.

This time of day, it would be deserted, he was sure. Before he reached the library door, Rachael caught up with him.

"Frank," she called his name, breathless from hurrying down the hall. "Frank, please stop."

He gritted his teeth. He didn't want to put on a happy face for the perky activity director. He just wanted to be alone.

She placed a hand on his shoulder and gently urged him to turn around.

Looking up into her sympathetic eyes, Frank lost control. Tears streamed down his face.

"What am I going to do?" he whispered, unable to speak aloud.

Without a word, Rachael knelt beside his chair and wrapped her arms around him. "I don't know, Frank, but I'm here to help you get through it."

He melted into her comforting embrace and allowed himself to cry, heedless of the fact that they were blocking half the hallway. He was unaware of the residents, who had finished with breakfast, as they skirted around, hugging the wall on the opposite side so as not to disturb them. He didn't notice when Brenda and Kent approached them, stopped, and stood beside Rachael, adding their comforting presence to hers.

Slowly, the tears ebbed, and he sat straighter, taking deep, hiccupy breaths. He looked up at Rachael and the others.

"I'm sorry," he murmured.

Rachael released her hold on him and sat back

on her heels.

"No need for apologies, Frank," she said gently.

"Thank you." He looked at Kent, then at Brenda. "Thank you." The simple words didn't feel like enough, but they were all he had.

No one said anything for a long moment.

Kent broke the silence. "We're here for you, Frank," he said, his voice full of compassion.

"I may not have arms to hug you," Brenda added, "but my ears work just fine, for when you want to talk."

Tears threatened to fall again, and Frank swiped at them almost angrily.

"Thank you both," he managed to say.

"Let's get you a ride to the hospital, shall we?" Rachael offered.

Frank nodded but couldn't say anything.

Thirty minutes later, he found himself wheeling into the front doors of Pine Valley Hospital. The receptionist greeted him, and he asked about Mike. She picked up the phone and punched a number. Talking softly, she made the inquiry, then hung up the phone.

"Your friend is still in the emergency room. Would you like to see him?"

"Yes, please!" Frank responded.

"Just take the left hallway…"

"I know the way," he interrupted, already turning his chair around. "Thank you," he called back over his shoulder.

Entering the too-familiar emergency room, he stopped a passing nurse. "Mike Hamblin?" he asked.

She pointed to a curtained-off area and hurried on her way.

Frank wheeled to the indicated curtain and stopped, suddenly filled with anxiety. A random air current blew the curtain back for a moment, and he caught a glimpse of Mike. The sight increased his fear but motivated him to enter.

Mike looked like a science experiment, with tubes and wires attached everywhere. Monitors blinked red, white, and green all around him. A semi-regular beeping interrupted the whooshing of the oxygen machine.

A nurse stood beside him, checking one of the monitors. She glanced up.

"Only a few minutes, sir," she said firmly. "We'll be transferring him to intensive care shortly." With that, she slipped through the curtain, and he was left alone with his friend.

Frank rolled up to the side of the bed and took Mike's hand.

Mike's face hadn't lost its ashen hue. In fact, it looked more gray than white in the harsh fluorescent light.

"Hang in there, Mike," Frank whispered, squeezing Mike's hand.

To his surprise, Mike squeezed back. It was weak, but it made Frank smile a little.

"You can hear me! That's wonderful!"

He stared into his friend's face, wishing he'd open his eyes.

"I talked with Kent, Brenda, and Rachael before I left. They said to tell you to hurry back. The place isn't the same without you." Frank's voice cracked on that last sentence, and he looked down, blinking hard to keep the tears from flowing again.

His roommate squeezed his hand again, and Frank looked into his face. Mike's eyes were open, watching Frank.

"Dnt… c… m…" he tried to say, his words muffled by the oxygen mask.

"Don't try to talk," Frank said. "You need your strength to get well."

Mike shook his head and lifted his free hand slowly toward the mask.

"Uh-uh. Leave that on. It's helping you breathe," Frank scolded as he gently pushed his arm back to the bed.

Again, Mike shook his head and tried to remove the mask.

"The nurse is going to kill you, if you take that off," Frank warned.

Mike pulled at the mask but could only shift it an inch or so. He dropped his hand, his expression a mixture of fatigue and frustration.

"It's okay, buddy," Frank said. "Whatever it is, it can wait."

Mike's eyebrows drew together into an unfamiliar angry scowl. He looked at Frank, but

Frank couldn't understand what his eyes were trying to say. After a moment, he sighed.

"All right, but just for a moment. You need this oxygen!"

He reached over and gently lifted the oxygen mask away, then looked into his friend's eyes.

"Don't be sad for me," Mike whispered. "I finally get to be with Sarah."

Instantly, tears filled Frank's eyes and slid down his cheeks.

"Let me go in peace," Mike continued. "True friendship, like true love, never ends."

"Who said that?" Frank asked with a sad smile.

"Mike Hamblin."

With that, Mike took a long, shuddery breath, and lay quiet.

Frank's eyes widened, and he quickly replaced the oxygen mask just as the monitors in the room went crazy. The doctor and nurses rushed in, and he backed out of the way, feeling in his heart that their ministrations would be in vain.

After only a few minutes, the doctor shook his head, and everyone stopped. It was a surreal moment for Frank, watching them begin to remove the wires and tubes.

The doctor turned to leave and noticed Frank for the first time.

"I'm sorry, son," he offered quietly.

Frank nodded his gratitude, then turned and wheeled out of the room. Numb with shock, he made his way to the hospital's chapel. He moved to a quiet corner and sat with his hands in his lap, his head hanging down, tears falling freely. After a few moments, he looked up at the cross standing tall in the front of the small room.

"Why, God?" he asked in a hoarse whisper. "Why?"

Staring out the window of his room, Frank didn't hear the soft knock at the door. He wasn't seeing anything out the window, either. He was lost in a dark, lonely world of grief.

The knock came again, a bit louder this time, but it still didn't penetrate Frank's sorrow.

After a moment, the door opened.

"Frank?"

Robyn's usually cheery voice was subdued, but it was enough to get Frank's attention, and he looked up.

"Robyn, I'm sorry, I didn't hear you," he responded, his voice sounding flat even to his own ears.

"That's okay," she said. "Are you up for visitors?"

"Visitors?" he repeated.

"Yeah, I brought someone with me," she said.

Stepping into the room behind Robyn, Janet peeked around her and smiled tentatively.

"We can come back another time, if you'd

rather," she offered in an almost whisper.

"No, I'm glad you came," Frank answered, realizing it was true. "Please come in. Or, we can go somewhere more comfortable to talk, if you'd like."

"This is fine," Robyn assured him as she sat on the edge of the bed.

Janet sat on the recliner, but Frank noticed she didn't relax.

There was an awkward silence, then they all spoke at once.

"How are you?" Robyn asked.

"I'm sorry…" Janet started.

"How's school?" Frank questioned.

That broke the ice, and they all chuckled weakly.

Frank decided to take the lead, not wanting to talk about what was really on his mind and heart.

"I was wondering how school is," he said.

"It's boring without you," Robyn quipped. "No one to tease or push around."

Frank shook his head and made a face at Robyn's intended pun.

"I'll be back, I promise. I just need a little time."

"Give yourself that time," Janet said softly. "Grief is hard."

Looking at her more closely, Frank was surprised to see her eyes glistening with unshed tears. Tempted to lighten the moment with a joke, he stopped himself.

"Thank you, I will," he replied, his voice huskier than he'd intended.

"Do you want to talk about Mike, or something else?" Robyn asked.

For the first time since his roommate's death, Frank found he really wanted to talk about him, to remember him with people who hadn't had the honor of knowing him.

"Thank you," he replied. "I'd like to tell you about him. Mike was the most amazing person I've ever met. He always had a quote for everything, and he wasn't afraid to give advice if you asked for it. Yet, he never intruded where he wasn't wanted. He had this way of sneaking up on me…"

The next hour was filled with laughter and tears as Frank relived his favorite memories of Mike. Robyn and Janet laughed and cried with him. When he reached the moment where he'd found him after the heart attack, Frank choked up and couldn't speak.

Janet reached over and laid her hand on his arm.

"You don't have to…" she began.

He looked at her and shook his head. "Yes, I do. I need to share it with someone or I'm going to drown in despair." He hesitated a moment and swallowed hard.

"Mike was my oar, my anchor, and my rudder. Whenever I was lost, he'd use one of his quotes to steer me in the right direction. His wise counsel would get me moving when I was stuck. Whenever

I was floundering, he would listen while I talked it out. I mean he'd really listen! Not just look at me and nod his head when it seemed appropriate. He was totally engaged in whatever I had to say. That's an incredible skill, you know?"

Robyn nodded. "Yes, it is, and a rare one, I've found."

"Right," Frank agreed. "Do you know what I've decided?"

"What?" Janet asked gently.

"I want to be like Mike when I grow up," Frank announced, then he slumped in his wheelchair. "I don't have his gift for remembering quotes, though."

"Was that the most important thing he offered you?" Robyn inquired.

Frank thought about it for a minute.

"No, I guess it wasn't," he mused. "The quotes got my attention, but what he offered was his full attention, his years of wisdom, and his loving heart."

"You can learn to give your full attention," Robyn observed, "and that kind of wisdom comes with age and experience."

"And you already have a loving heart," Janet offered shyly.

That caught Frank off-guard. "Why do you say that?" he asked, truly wanting to know.

Janet ducked her head, then looked sideways at him before responding.

"Well, you left me your plate of food at the

park," she said simply.

"You saw that?" he asked, his eyebrows raised.

"I did. I was watching from the trees. I saw Mrs. Whitney leave the water and was about to run out to get it when you wheeled up to the bench and left your plate there."

"Well…" Frank started, feeling uncomfortable.

"You have no way to know that between what Mrs. Whitney left and what you left, I wasn't hungry for the first time in weeks. That food fed me for almost a week."

"A week?!" Frank was shocked. "But it was just a burger and some potato salad."

"Only a burger to you," Janet said with a little smile, "but a life-altering act of kindness to me."

"I don't understand."

"That was the beginning of a new life for me," she replied. "I won't go into the details now, but just knowing that there were people in this town like you and Mrs. Whitney gave me the hope I desperately needed. Thank you for that."

Frank didn't know what to say. It hadn't been a big deal to him to leave his food. He hadn't been hungry anyway. To discover that it had meant so much to this woman was more than he could wrap his head around.

"On that note," Robyn said after a few moments of silence, "we'd probably better get going. Will we see you in school Monday?"

"Probably," Frank answered, still trying to wrap her head around what he'd just heard.

"Good!" Robyn stood and moved toward the door.

Janet sat for a moment, then she reached into her pocket, pulled out a little piece of paper, and pressed it into his hand.

"What's this?" he asked looking down at it.

"My friend's phone number," she replied. "You can reach me there to set up those tutoring sessions… that is, if you still want my help."

"I certainly do," Frank said sincerely. "Thank you!"

When the women had gone, Frank stared at the scribbled phone number in his hand. He was touched and pleased that Janet had trusted him enough to share it with him. Somehow, he had a feeling that had taken a huge leap of faith for her. With a silent vow to never betray her trust, he wheeled over and wrote the number in his little address book. On a whim, he drew a smiley face beside it.

Chapter 23

Frank breathed heavily as he replaced the hand weights on the rack. He was sweating and more than a little out of breath. Physically, it felt good to push himself, but it hadn't done much to lighten his mood. Frowning, he turned his wheelchair and headed for the door. He pushed the wheels hard and nearly ran into Kevin, who'd just walked in.

"Whoa, buddy!" the physical therapist warned. "You're driving a deadly weapon there. What's your hurry?"

"No hurry," Frank replied. "Just not watching where I was going. Sorry."

He pushed his chair back and tried to go around his friend, but Kevin stepped in front of him.

"Hold on, Frank. There's obviously something bothering you. Want to talk?"

"Nope."

Kevin raised an eyebrow. "I'm not buying it. What's going on?"

Frank looked up and scowled. "I said I don't want to talk about it."

"Ah, so there *is* something!" Kevin exclaimed triumphantly.

"No, there's not!"

Kevin folded his arms and tapped his foot, waiting.

"Leave it alone, Kev," Frank warned.

Kevin pursed his lips and cocked his head. When Frank didn't say anything else, he gave a quick nod.

"Okay, I get it. How about we go to the dining room for a cup of coffee? You don't have to say a word. I just want a little company. Will you join me?"

Frank sighed. "You're not going to let this go, are you?"

"What?" Kevin feigned surprise. "I said you didn't have to talk. Just come have a cup of coffee with me. I think there may even be some cinnamon rolls left from breakfast."

"Fine, but I'm not talking!"

"Sounds good to me."

As Kevin turned to lead the way, Frank was sure he caught a little grin on his physical therapist's face.

They moved silently down the hall and into the dining room. Without speaking, they filled two cups and put two cinnamon rolls on a plate. Frank balanced the plate on his lap and pushed the wheels on his chair while Kevin carried the coffee to a nearby table.

Still silent, they began munching the slightly stale rolls and sipping their coffee. After three bites and sips, Frank looked at Kevin.

"What am I doing here, Kev?" he asked.

"Looks like you're eating a cinnamon roll and drinking coffee," Kevin quipped.

"I'm serious," Frank replied. "What am I doing with my life? I eat, I sleep, I go to class, but none of it seems like it's going to get me anywhere. I just can't see living this way for the rest of my life."

"How are your classes going?" Kevin asked.

"Not as well as I'd like," Frank admitted. "My eye-hand coordination isn't great, my memory sucks, and my math skills are nearly non-existent. Besides, who's going to hire a CAD drafter who has MS?"

"No way to tell at this point," Kevin replied, "but you won't know until you graduate and start job hunting. I get the feeling that school isn't all that's bugging you."

Frank was silent for a few moments, staring into his cup. When he spoke, his voice shook with pent up emotion.

"No, it's not. Things just aren't the same without Mike around. I told some friends the other day that when he died, I lost my oar, my rudder, and my anchor. I'm floating in the middle of this huge ocean with no way to move forward, no way to steer, and no way to keep from being tossed around by any wave that comes along."

"Sounds a little scary."

"Not scary so much as lonely," Frank confessed.

"How have your other roommates been?" Kevin asked.

Frank took a moment to think about how he could be diplomatic but still convey his frustration with the string of roommates he'd had.

"Well," he finally said, "most of them are three times my age and have no interest in chatting or becoming friends. I don't think the dividing curtain has been open since Mike died... except once."

"Once?"

"Yeah, I had a roommate for one whole weekend who was quite the opposite. He decided to open the curtain and keep me up all night telling me every single experience he'd ever had in his entire life."

"Well, that sounds interesting, at least," Kevin responded with a grin.

"You'd think so, wouldn't you?" Frank replied, making a sour face. "Let's just say his life wasn't exactly exciting. The most thrilling thing he told me was about the time he bought a new milk cow who had twin calves in the spring of 1943, which turned out to be the wettest spring they'd had in Kansas in twenty years."

Kevin faked a cough to cover up a chuckle.

"Exactly my point," Frank continued, choosing to ignore his friend's amusement at his expense. Well, maybe it would be amusing to him in a few years. Right now, it was just frustrating.

Kevin got control of himself and sat back in his chair, looking thoughtful.

"So, why don't you move out?"

Frank looked shocked. "What?"

"Move out. Get a ground level apartment and live life on your own terms for a change. You're pretty self-sufficient now. You can take care of your basic needs. You might need help once in a while for large grocery trips, or deep cleaning tasks, but I think you'd be just fine living alone."

Suddenly, Frank's mind was racing. Could he really do it? Could he actually move out and make it on his own? What about money? What about getting to and from doctor appointments? What about…

"It's something to consider," Kevin continued. "I can see you have a lot of questions, so let's just take this one step at a time. We can talk with the Social Security people when they come to town next week about how the finances would all work. Then, we can start looking for a place for you. After that, everything else will fall into place."

"But…" Frank started.

"No 'buts' just yet, my friend," Kevin interrupted. "Let's just see what the possibilities are."

"That makes sense," Frank admitted. "You've sure given me a lot to think about!"

Kevin grinned. "Good! Thinking is better than moping!"

"Hey!" Frank tried to look offended, but he ended up with a silly scowl instead. "Thanks, Kev. I think there may be hope for me, after all."

"There's always hope, Frank," Kevin replied. "Always."

The next two weeks flew by as Frank and Kevin went through the steps necessary for him to move out of Shady Pines. They met with a young woman from the Social Security office, who assured him it would not affect his Social Security if he lived on his own. In fact, since he'd have control of his own money, he might actually benefit financially from the move.

They talked with his doctor, who supported the decision, and the financial department at Shady Pines. Then, they were finally ready to begin looking for an apartment.

That's when things got tough.

"I'm sorry, sir," the middle-aged woman said, shaking her head. "I need three recent references before I can rent to you."

"But I've been in…" Frank started.

"I know, 'Shady Pines for the past sixteen months'," the woman interrupted. "I'm sorry. Rules are rules." With that, she closed the door firmly, leaving them on the front porch.

Frank growled. "She didn't even let us see the

room!"

"I know," Kevin replied, putting a reassuring hand on Frank's shoulder. "Obviously, this wasn't the right place."

"I don't think there is a right place," Frank complained. "Everyone takes one look at my wheels and slams the door in my face! It's useless!"

"Don't give up so easily," Kevin encouraged. "There are still three places on your list."

"I'm done," Frank announced. "I'm just done."

"Okay," Kevin said with a nod, "we can stop for today. What say we get a bite to eat before we head back to Shady Pines?"

"Whatever," Frank responded with a shrug and a shake of his head.

Making their way back to Kevin's car, Frank felt discouraged and frustrated. Why did it seem that the MS was getting in the way of everything he wanted to do? He couldn't be a machinist anymore. He wasn't making much progress in school. He'd certainly never have a relationship, or even a date, at this rate. Now, it seemed no one was willing to rent to a man in a wheelchair. He'd be stuck in a nursing home with an endless string of unbearable roommates for the rest of his life. Not an appealing prospect!

After putting Frank's wheelchair in the trunk, Kevin climbed into the driver's seat.

"Where to? What are you hungry for?" he asked.

"Don't care," Frank muttered.

Kevin watched him for a moment, then turned the key in the ignition. "Okay, buddy. You don't offer an opinion, you take what I choose."

Frank rolled his eyes. He truly didn't care. He looked out the window as Kevin drove, but he wasn't really seeing anything. That is, until a movement down a side street caught his eye.

"Wait!" he cried. "Kevin, back up. I want you to turn down Elm Street."

"Oh? What's up?" Kevin asked as he pulled over to the right side of the street and then made a quick U-turn.

"I think I just saw Brent fall off his bike!"

"Oh, man!"

Kevin turned down Elm and drove half a block. Sure enough, they spotted Brent's bicycle, upside down in a ditch, its wheels still spinning. Kevin slammed on the brakes, jumped out and raced over.

Frank sat watching, feeling more and more helpless. He should be helping pull the bike out of the ditch! He should be helping rescue Brent! He shouldn't be stuck here in the car with useless legs, unable to do anything to help!

Kevin had Brent up on the ditch bank, trying to convince him to lie back and wait for the paramedics to check him over. Brent was shaking his head and trying to stand up.

Finally, Frank had enough. He rolled down his window and called out.

"Hey, Brent!"

The middle-aged man looked over at him.

"Remember when you rescued me after my wheelchair got stuck?"

Brent grinned and nodded.

"Good. Well, now I want you to do me another favor. I want you to let the paramedics check you over to be sure you're safe to ride that bike of yours. Okay?"

Brent hesitated, then nodded, relaxing back onto the grassy bank.

Frank couldn't help but smile a little at the relieved expression on Kevin's face.

At least I still have my voice, he thought. *That's something.*

At that moment, he noticed that they were only a couple of blocks from his house. Well, what used to be his house. He'd sold it last summer when it looked like he'd be living at Shady Pines for the rest of his life. He wondered if the new owners had changed it much.

His thoughts wandered for the next little while as the paramedics arrived, looked Brent over, and declared he was fine. He watched as Brent got back on his bicycle and started off, waving and grinning like nothing had happened.

"That's one lucky man," Kevin observed as he got back in the car.

"Yeah," Frank agreed. "Hey, Kev, before we go to eat, could we drive by my old place? I just want to see if the new owners have changed it at all."

"Sure, buddy. No problem."

A few moments later, they were parked across the street from Frank's house. It looked much the same, except there were two new flower beds, one on each side of the front steps.

"Flowers look nice," Frank said, feeling a little sad. "I never thought to put flowers in."

"They are pretty," Kevin agreed, "but it's been my experience that flowers are a lot of work. Pulling weeds, spraying for bugs, cutting off dead blossoms. You know the drill."

"Not really, but I wish I'd tried it, at least."

"Who knows?" Kevin said with a shrug. "You may get a chance someday."

"Yeah, right," Frank replied skeptically, then jumped as someone tapped on his window.

"Frank?" the old woman's voice called through the glass. "Is that you?"

"Mrs. Baumgartner!" Frank exclaimed, rolling down his window. "You look great!"

"Well, I do declare! You are a sight for sore eyes!"

Frank's grin broadened. "You always say that!"

"This time, I mean it!" Mrs. Baumgartner replied. She bent down a bit and peered in at Kevin. "Who's your handsome driver?"

Frank laughed. "This is Kevin, my physical therapist and friend. Kevin, this is Mrs. Baumgartner, my longtime neighbor and friend."

Kevin leaned over and smiled at the old woman. "Nice to meet you, ma'am."

"Good to meet you, too, young man," she replied.

"How's Ted?" Frank asked.

"Not much change. He has his good days and bad ones. Still has the same great attitude, though," she bragged, then glanced across the street. "You come to see the old place?"

Frank nodded. "Yes. I was feeling a bit homesick."

"You still living over at Shady Pines?" she asked.

"Yes, but I'm thinking of moving out on my own."

"Are you?" she asked, her eyes brightening. "What kind of place would you be looking for?"

"Something on the small side, but with wide doorways for my chair," Frank replied, "and it has to be single level. No stairs, inside or out."

A slow smile crept over Mrs. Baumgartner's face and crinkled the corners of her eyes.

"I may just have the place for you," she announced. "Hold on a minute. I'll go get the key."

After a surprisingly short time, she returned with a door key. "It's easy to find, right on Main Street. There's a green door and a brown one between the flower shop and the bakery. This key fits the green door. Go look it over and let me know what you think."

"Wow! Thanks, Mrs. Baumgartner!" Frank

exclaimed. "We'll do just that."

Sure enough, the tiny apartment proved to be perfect. There was no step up from the sidewalk to get inside, the doorways were wide enough for his wheelchair, and everything was on ground level. Frank didn't even mind the checkerboard tile on the floor, even though Kevin said looking at it made him dizzy. After touring the place, they drove back to Mrs. Baumgartner's house and sealed the deal.

After leaving Mrs. Baumgartner's, they stopped at the A&W for a burger.

"How do you feel now, buddy?" Kevin asked.

"I feel great! Better than great!" Frank replied. "I can't believe we found the perfect place!"

Kevin laughed. "And all because you noticed Brent falling into that ditch."

Frank felt bemused. "You're right. If I hadn't been watching out the window, we'd have come straight here and would have missed talking with Mrs. Baumgartner."

"Just goes to show you, opportunity is everywhere. The key is to develop the vision to see it."

"Now you sound like Mike!" Frank laughed, and Kevin grinned.

As they finished their meal, Frank felt better than he had in a long time.

Time for a new adventure, he thought.

Chapter 24

"Why not?" Janet asked for the third time, nervously fingering the computer mouse on her table.

"Because I really don't have that much stuff," Frank answered, trying not to feel irritated at her insistence. "Kevin is going to pick me up tomorrow, put my box and my suitcase in his car, and drive me over. Mrs. Baumgartner has arranged to have the apartment furnished, so I don't have any furniture to move. It's going to be quick and easy. I appreciate your offer, but I just don't need the help."

"How are you going to hang up your clothes when you get there?" she asked. "I could at least do that."

"All my clothes will go in the dresser, and I can reach the drawers just fine."

"What about groceries?" she pressed. "Can I pick up some groceries for you?"

"No, thank you," he replied, shaking his head. "Kevin is taking me shopping on the way to the apartment."

"Isn't there something I can do to help?" she pleaded. "I really want to."

"I appreciate it, Janet, but I don't need anything," he insisted.

Finally, Janet stopped, looked down at her hands and just sat. She took a couple of deep breaths, and Frank wondered if she was trying to keep from crying. He glanced around the classroom and was grateful there were only two other people in the room; Robyn, who was sitting at the computer on the other side of him, and a geeky-looking guy in the far corner wearing headphones.

When Frank had told Janet that he was moving into his own place, she seemed to be as excited as he was. She'd said before that she didn't think he belonged in that nursing home in the first place. She praised him often for being so independent. In fact, she'd really opened up since he and Robyn had first invited her to lunch. Maybe it was the tutoring sessions. She seemed to enjoy helping him figure out the math stuff, and he thought he might actually be progressing.

So, why was she upset that he didn't need her help now?

"Can I bring you a housewarming gift?" she finally asked.

"What for?" Frank was truly puzzled. "It's

just a little apartment, a place to lay my head. That's all. Not much room for any trinkets or doodads. Thanks, anyway."

"Fine. Good luck with your move." Janet pushed back from the computer table, grabbed her bookbag, and started for the door.

For a moment, he admired the way her jeans looked on her without the old sweater she used to wear. His admiration was cut short, however when she stopped and turned back around.

"Frank Berglund, I think you are a prideful man!" she announced with more spunk than he'd ever seen in her.

"Wait, what?" he asked. "Prideful? What makes you think that?"

"I think you are so proud of the fact that you can move into your own place, that you refuse to allow anyone else to help you," she ranted. "Did you ever think that maybe you'd be doing *me* a favor by letting me help a little? Did you ever think that maybe I *need* to do good deeds once in a while? Did you ever think that maybe I *want* to help you? Did you ever think that by refusing, you might be hurting my feelings and denying me blessings? Did you?"

With that, she turned on her heel and stormed out of the classroom.

Frank watched her, feeling bewildered. He knew he was right. He didn't need her help. He was perfectly capable, and with Kevin to drive him, he'd be just fine. Surely, she could see that.

Then, Ruth's philosophy came to mind. Allow others to help you. His frown deepened and his brow furrowed.

"Nice," Robyn commented as she closed her book.

"What?" Frank looked over at his friend. "What's her deal? Why'd she go off like that?"

Robyn shook her head and grinned. "You really don't know, do you? Are you really that clueless?"

"Apparently," he replied, raising one eyebrow. "What am I missing?"

"It wasn't about you needing help, Frank," Robyn answered as she shut off her computer. Turning to face him, she continued, "It was about doing something for you, seeing you in your new place, and mostly, spending time with you."

"Spending time with me? Why?"

Robyn cocked her head. "You really don't see it? She likes you! As in, she'd like to spend more time with you. A lot more time. Like the rest of her life kind of time."

Frank's jaw dropped.

"Like she wants to be my girlfriend kind of time?"

Robyn nodded.

Frank blew out a long breath.

"I had no idea she felt that way."

"Obviously," Robyn shrugged. "So, what are you going to do about it?"

"What can I do? I've hurt her feelings, and

she'll probably never want to talk to me again." He didn't know why, but that thought created a heavy, dark place where his heart should have been.

"I don't think it's that bad," Robyn said reassuringly. "Unless you choose to ignore the situation."

"What do you suggest?"

"I suggest you go find her! Don't let her just run out without following her. Apologize for your thick head and ask her to bring you dinner tomorrow night."

"Dinner?"

"Dinner," Robyn repeated with a decisive nod. "She'll jump at the chance and will forgive you anything."

"Really?"

"Trust me, Frank. It'll work."

Frank looked at the door and then back at Robyn. "If you're sure," he said hesitantly.

"I'm sure. Go!" Robyn stood, grabbed the handles on the back of his wheelchair and pushed him toward the door.

Frank took it from there and pushed himself out the door into the hall. He looked right, then left, but didn't see any sign of Janet. The hallway was empty. Taking a chance, he wheeled to his right and glanced in every alcove between his classroom and the north door at the end of the hall. No luck. Turning back, he repeated the process all the way to the south end. Still no luck.

Now what?

Maybe he should call her when he got back to Shady Pines. He could apologize over the phone and ask her to bring him dinner. Hopefully, that would do it. He wheeled himself out the main doors and down to the bus stop, feeling the relief that comes from a decision firmly made. This crisis could be averted, he was sure.

When he arrived in his room, he wheeled straight for the phone. Dialing the phone number Janet had given him, he counted the rings. One. Two. Three. He pursed his lips. Four. Five. Six. He frowned. Seven. Eight. Nine. With a sigh, he replaced the receiver. He'd have to try again later. Maybe after dinner. With that thought, he threw his few belongings into the box waiting on his dresser and headed to the dining room.

He wasn't too surprised when he pushed the dining room door open and everyone yelled surprise. He pretended to be and was touched that so many residents and staff wanted to say goodbye and wish him well. It was a great going-away party! He felt a little sad to be leaving so many friends here. But the adventure of living on his own again outweighed any melancholy.

As he finished his nightly routine and transferred from his chair into bed, he smiled to himself. Tomorrow was going to be a great day! Closing his eyes, he tried to imagine what it would be like. But his happy thoughts were interrupted by the image of Janet's tear-stained face as she ran out of the classroom.

He opened his eyes and looked at the clock. 11 p.m. It was too late to call her tonight. He'd have to do it first thing in the morning. Yup. That's what he'd do. With a deep breath and a little sigh, he drifted off to sleep.

The next morning, Frank woke up feeling bright and cheery. He hurried through his morning routine, checked that he hadn't left anything in the bathroom or drawers, then waited a bit impatiently for Kevin to show up.

Half an hour later, Kevin poked his head in the doorway.

"Are you ready for this?" he asked.

"Have been for thirty minutes!" Frank exclaimed. "Let's get this show on the road!"

Kevin laughed and grabbed the box off the dresser.

"You got the suitcase, buddy?"

"Got it!" Frank declared as he pulled the suitcase onto his lap.

Wheeling down the hall, he grinned and waved as everyone lined up to say goodbye, even though most had said goodbye the night before.

I feel like Brent, waving and grinning, he thought.

The grocery trip was uneventful, yet exciting somehow. He'd never appreciated how fulfilling it was to be able to stock his own kitchen cupboards before. No longer would he have to eat whatever someone else served. He could make his own choices, cook his own food, and clean up his own dishes. Well, the last part wasn't too exciting, but still…

As Kevin emptied the grocery bags into the refrigerator and cupboards, Frank put his clothes away. He'd been right. All his clothes fit into the dresser drawers nicely. No need for hangers in the closet.

"I'm finished in the kitchen," Kevin announced. "Anything else you need?"

"Nope," Frank replied, shaking his head. "I think I'm good!"

"Want me to rustle up some lunch before I go?"

"Are you kidding me? I've been looking forward to cooking for myself for two weeks now!"

Kevin raised his hands in surrender. "Understood. It's all yours, buddy. Enjoy!"

Frank saw his friend to the door. When the front door was closed, he turned his wheelchair around and surveyed his new digs. He nodded in satisfaction.

Yes, this will do nicely, he thought.

Just then, his stomach rumbled, and he laughed. Kevin was right, it was lunchtime. He made himself a peanut butter and jelly sandwich, poured a glass of milk, and only spilled a few drops as he transferred it to the table.

"Good thing the kitchen is so small," he said aloud, then chuckled. "Talking to yourself already, Berglund? This doesn't bode well!"

After lunch, he cleaned up the few dishes,

then wheeled into the little living room. Picking up a book from the coffee table, he opened it.

"Chapter One," he read. It didn't take long for him to get lost in the pages. He'd read *The Hobbit* many times as a teenager, but this was the first time since his diagnosis. His double vision made it a bit of a challenge, and he had to keep stopping to refocus, but the story kept his attention anyway.

Several hours later, he realized he had a headache. He rubbed his eyes, then looked out the living room window. It was dusk, which surprised him. Time sure flies when you've got a good book!

He put the book back on the coffee table and wheeled into the kitchen. What to make for dinner. Hm. He opened a lower cupboard door and saw a box of macaroni and cheese. Yes! Chili-mac would hit the spot. Opening other lower cupboards, he looked for the can of chili he remembered buying. He didn't find it, though.

I wonder where Kevin put it, he thought. He checked all the lower cupboards again. No chili. Glancing up, he cocked his head warily. Surely Kevin wouldn't have put it up there! He was smarter than that, right?

Frank looked in the corner where he'd put the broom. Reaching over, he grabbed it, slid his hands down to the bristle end, and hooked the broom handle into the cupboard handle. Pulling gently, he was able to open the cupboard door. Sure enough, on the bottom shelf sat the can of chili, and a few other canned items.

Maneuvering his wheelchair as close as he could to the counter, he reached up and tried to grab the can. It was about five inches out of his reach. Glancing at the broom, Frank lifted it up, bristles first, and tried to push the chili can off the shelf. The broom slipped and pushed the can further back.

Dang!

Attempting to think outside the box, Frank tried to manipulate the stick end of the broom behind the can. He only succeeded in pushing it farther back.

"All right, Berglund," he said aloud, "Time to get serious. If you're going to live on your own, you've got to figure this out."

He sat back and thought for a few moments. The only way he could see to retrieve the can was to pull himself up to a standing position and grab it. He could do this. The counter was sturdy, his arms were strong. Piece of cake!

Leaning down, he lifted his feet off the footrests and onto the floor. Then, he opened the silverware drawer a little and grabbed the edge of the counter, thumbs on top, fingers underneath. He took a deep breath and pulled, being careful to pull equally with both hands. Slowly, slowly, he felt his body lift off the wheelchair seat as he rose almost to a standing position. A couple of times, he thought his legs were going to give out, but he kept pulling until he was fully upright.

Yes!

He looked up at the offending can, gratified that it was at eye level now. Carefully, he let go of the counter with his right hand and reached for the chili. Almost. Just another inch. He leaned into the counter, hoping to reach the can. As he leaned, his hips closed the silverware drawer, slamming it against his fingers. Instinctively, he yanked his hand out with a yelp.

With nothing holding him up, both legs collapsed, and he felt himself falling. Flailing his arms, he grabbed at the cupboard, the counter, the drawer, and finally his chair. The chair rolled away, and he saw the counter edge coming before his forehead hit.

"Frank! Frank!"

The voice seemed so far away, yet so insistent.

"Frank! Wake up!"

His head was pounding. He just wanted to sleep.

"Frank Berglund!" she demanded as she shook his shoulder. "If you don't open your eyes, I'm going to call an ambulance."

"Amb…ln…s?" he mumbled.

"I hear your voice, now let's see your eyes," she insisted.

"Jn… t?"

"Yes, it's Janet. Open your eyes!"

Frank took a shaky breath and tried to open his eyes. Slowly, they obeyed, and he found himself looking into the face of a very determined woman.

She nodded. "Good."

Then, he was blinded by a flashlight shining in each eye.

"Equal and reactive. Good," she declared. "I think you'll live."

Frank blinked a few times, trying to focus. "How…?"

"I heard you yell," she answered.

"Why…?"

"Why am I here?" she asked with a wry grin. "Because I felt badly about how I reacted to your desire to do this yourself. I shouldn't have been such a pest about it, and I definitely shouldn't have stormed off like I did. I'm sorry."

Frank blinked again, realized he was lying on the floor, and tried to sit up.

"Whoa there, cowboy," Janet said, pushing him back down. "Give yourself a few minutes, then if you're feeling up to it, we'll sit you up. Let's just take this slow and easy, okay?"

Frank closed his eyes and took a few deep breaths. No pain in his ribs or back. That was good. After a moment, he looked up at her and nodded carefully.

"I think I'm ready to sit up," he said.

Janet helped him into a sitting position, bracing his back against her.

"How does that feel?" she asked.

"Everything feels fine except my head," he admitted.

"So, good and bad, huh?"

"Yeah."

They sat in silence for a few more minutes.

"Frank?"

"Yeah?"

"How are we going to get you back in your chair?" she asked, worry in her voice. "I don't think I'm strong enough to lift you."

"You don't have to," he reassured her. "If you'll push my chair so it's against my right side, I'll pull myself up."

"What?!" Janet looked incredulous.

"Ever since I fell last time," he answered, "I've been working out, strengthening my arms. If the chair is in the right position and the brakes are on, I can pull myself into it."

"Really? Show me," she challenged as she stood.

Rolling the chair into position as Frank directed her, bracing it against the refrigerator, she set the brakes and stood back.

Frank grabbed the sides of the seat, took a deep breath and pulled, twisting his body as his arms lifted him off the ground, sliding with a soft grunt into the wheelchair.

Janet's eyes widened and her jaw dropped.

"That's the most incredible thing I've ever seen!" she exclaimed.

"See?" he gloated. "I'm not so useless after all!"

She frowned. "I never said you were useless."

"I didn't say you did," he responded. "I'm sorry."

"It's okay," she said, looking away. "I always seem to be saying the wrong things. I'm the one who's sorry."

"You have nothing to be sorry for, Janet," Frank said softly. "You only wanted to help. You were right. I am prideful, and I shouldn't be. I should have been more grateful for your offer to help."

Janet looked at him with a tenderness he'd never seen before.

He was struck by how beautiful she was. Her hair flowed softly and was the color of caramel. Not the mousy brown he remembered. Her eyes were gentle, blue as the summer sky. Her mouth curved in a small, but rather enticing smile.

"Is there something I can help with now?" she asked gently, interrupting his pleasant observations of her.

He looked around the kitchen and saw the silverware drawer upside down on the floor, knives, forks, and spoons scattered all around it. The chili can, along with several other cans, had rolled into the corner.

"Could you help me straighten up in here?" he replied with a grin. "I'm such a slob!"

"I believe it," Janet teased as she leaned down

to pick up the drawer.

He chuckled and marveled at the same time. She never would have teased him before.

The next few minutes were spent setting things to rights, then together, they cooked up some chili-mac. It was all very comfortable, and Frank found himself wondering why he hadn't accepted her help when she'd offered.

As Janet cleared the table, Robyn's words came into Frank's mind.

"She'd like to spend more time with you. A lot more time. Like the rest of her life kind of time."

I wonder, he thought.

Chapter 25

Frank grinned as Janet pointed out the Karmann Ghia he was about to show her.

"Is that it?" she asked.

"Right!" he exclaimed. "You've been paying attention."

She giggled behind him, continuing to push his wheelchair over the path between the old cars.

He'd always loved the Pine Valley Car Show and was grateful she'd agreed to come with him this year. She didn't even seem to mind pushing his chair over the bumpy fairgrounds grass.

Stopping in front of the Ghia, she moved around beside him as he began telling her the history of the car and why it was his favorite.

"I'm going to own one, someday!" he declared. "I'll restore it like new and paint it blight blue."

" 'Blight blue'?" she repeated, laughing.

He loved her laugh!

"Yup," he confirmed with a definitive nod. "Blight blue. It's like a robin's egg blue, but brighter."

"There's no such color," she protested.

"Of course, there is!" he insisted. "I see it on semi-trucks all the time."

"You'll have to show me sometime," she said with a chuckle.

"I will!"

They continued perusing the lines of cars as the afternoon sun grew hotter. Finally, she stopped near a bench and sat down.

"I'm done!" she declared. "This August heat is killing me."

"I'm sure it doesn't help that you have to push me around in this thing," he responded with a frown.

"Oh, I don't mind that," she said, then grinned. "At least, I wouldn't mind it if it were cooler."

Frank chuckled. "Fair enough. What if we go find something cold to drink? Maybe even something to eat, too, since it's nearly lunch time."

"You're on!" Janet declared, standing up.

It took a few minutes to make their way back to the concessions building. As Janet opened the double doors, a blast of cool air hit them, and they sighed in unison, then laughed.

"So, what strikes your fancy?" Frank asked. "Corn dogs, pulled pork sandwich, or Navajo taco?"

"Definitely Navajo taco," she replied firmly. "I never come to events like this without getting one."

Chuckling, Frank pointed down an aisle between the vendor booths. "I think they were selling them over that way."

Just then, Frank noticed an elderly man in front of them. He was trying to carry a plate of food, a drink cup, and a cane. Before Frank could offer to help, a young boy ran by, bumping into the man. The plate went flying and the cup fell, spilling its contents all over the man and the floor. The man nearly lost his balance, as well.

Without a word, Frank grabbed the wheels of his chair and propelled himself forward, coming to a stop beside the gentleman.

"Are you all right, sir?" he asked, touching the man's elbow.

"I… I think so." The man's voice quavered, though, showing how shaken up he was.

"Can I help you?"

At that point, the man looked at Frank and sighed. "I don't think so, young man. I think I'll just give up and go home. These events are meant for young people, not for old codgers like me."

"Nonsense!" Frank declared. "I'm sure you remember driving many of these cars in your day."

A grin stole across the old man's face. "I sure do! And I enjoyed every one of them!"

"I'll bet you did!"

Just then, Janet appeared by Frank's side.

"Excuse me, sir," she said quietly. "I believe you had a cheeseburger, fries, and root beer, didn't you?"

"How did you know?" the man asked, surprised.

Janet smiled sweetly as she glanced down at a fresh plate of food and shrugged. "The girl at the Burger Barn booth remembered you."

"But…" he began.

"Shall we find a safer place for you to eat?" she asked. "I'll carry these for you…" Then, she looked down at Frank. "That is, if you can wheel yourself, good sir?"

"Of course, I can!" Frank declared.

As they made their way to a table not far from the Navajo taco booth, Frank was in awe of the change in Janet. Gone was the timid, frightened, homeless woman he'd first seen at the Labor Day picnic. Here was a sweet, giving lady with a laugh that could brighten the darkest day. When confronted with someone who needed something… anything… she was the first to help, usually without being asked. Frank wasn't sure what had made the difference. He determined to ask her when he had the chance.

Once they'd made sure the gentleman was settled, they ordered their own food and joined him when it was ready.

"My name's Frank, and this is my friend, Janet."

"Nice to meet you, my name's Mel. I can't

thank you enough for coming to my rescue. Buying my lunch was above and beyond what anyone could expect."

"Not at all," Janet replied, a trace of her former shyness peeking through.

"Are you here alone, Mel?" Frank asked.

"Well, I was supposed to meet my brother here, but he seems to have stood me up."

Frank frowned a little. "I hope he's okay."

"I'm sure he is," Mel replied. "He's just a little slower these days, like me."

They chit-chatted for a few minutes, then Mel glanced at the open door a few yards away.

"There he is!" He grinned and called, "Carl! Over here!"

Frank turned in his chair and looked up in time to see his old friend, Carl, coming toward them, holding the handle of a guide dog's harness. Frank grinned as the pair approached their table.

"Mel!" Carl said as he stepped nearer. "I'm sorry to keep you waiting."

"No problem," Mel answered. "These nice young people have taken good care of me. Frank, Janet, I'd like you to meet my brother, Carl."

Carl held out his hand, but Frank noticed that Carl seemed to look just past him. Realization dawned, and he reached out to take Carl's hand, grasping it firmly.

"We've met," Frank said with a smile. "First, at the bus stop where I nearly bowled you and your puppy over. What was her name? Betsy?"

Carl laughed as he felt for the chair next to Janet. "Close, it was Bessie."

"Oh, right. What's this one's name?"

"This is Hero," Carl answered, reaching down to pat the chocolate lab's head as he settled under the table at their feet. Hero's tail thumped happily. "I believe we met again when you were trying to learn how to navigate the real world in your wheelchair."

"That's right!" Frank exclaimed. "We do seem to meet in strange places, don't we?"

"Those sound like fascinating stories," Janet interjected with a smile and a twinkle in her eye. "I'd love to hear them."

"They are," Frank said. "Carl and I have been running into each other…"

"Only literally the first time," Carl interrupted with a laugh.

"Right," Frank chuckled. "Anyway, we've seen each other off and on for the past couple of years. Carl trains guide dog puppies."

"You do?" Janet asked, surprised.

"Well, I used to," Carl confirmed. "I've retired from that now." He went on to share some of his experiences with those puppies, Mel adding in his own memories of each one.

The next hour was spent chatting amiably and catching up. Finally, after Janet had procured some funnel cakes for dessert, Frank asked the question that had plagued him since Carl arrived.

"If you don't mind me asking, Carl, I'd love

to hear what's been going on with you."

Chuckling, Carl replied. "Is that your polite way of asking how I came to be blind?"

"Well, yes," Frank admitted. "When you walked up with Hero, I thought maybe you'd graduated to the actual guide dog training."

Carl smiled indulgently. "Not exactly. Shortly after the last time we ran into each other, I was in a car accident that left me partially paralyzed and completely blind."

"Oh, no! I'm so sorry!" Frank exclaimed.

"Thank you," Carl smiled and nodded. "The rest of the story is the best part. I had just finished training a puppy and was returning from delivering him to the training center when the accident happened. I was pretty angry for a while. Oh, I went through the physical therapy to regain most of my mobility but resisted the training they offered to help me function without my sight.

"Then, one day, I was sitting on my front porch, feeling sorry for myself when I heard someone come up the walk. I called out, asking who was there. Turns out, it was my supervisor in the guide dog puppy training program. We visited for a bit, then he told me why he was there. He wanted me to come and be matched up with a guide dog. I argued with him, but he was insistent. Finally, he wore me down, and I agreed to come.

"That first night was awful. I was in unfamiliar surroundings and was scared to death. I didn't know what I was doing there. I just wanted to be at home on my front porch feeling sorry for myself. That had become comfortable to me.

"The next morning, I was introduced to my guide dog… the very last puppy I had trained before my accident!"

He reached down and scratched behind Hero's ear. "Hero and I are inseparable now."

"What? Hero was the puppy you trained?" Frank asked, amazed.

"Yes. He's my reward, my friend, my buddy, my… hero."

"That's a beautiful story," Janet said, her voice husky with emotion.

"I agree," Carl replied. "Who would have guessed that I'd be puppy training my own guide dog?"

"Just goes to show that you never know what life will bring," Mel chimed in. "For example, when I agreed to meet Carl here, I had no idea that we'd be sharing lunch with such a charming and kind couple!"

"Oh, we're not…" Janet and Frank started in unison. They looked at each other, then laughed a little.

Carl cocked his head and pursed his lips. He looked as though he was about to say something, but just smiled instead.

Embarrassed, Frank tried to change the subject. "So, I take it you gentlemen haven't toured the cars yet?"

"Not yet," Mel reported. "We're supposed to

walk through after lunch."

"I recommend that you take special notice of the Karmann Ghia," Frank suggested. "The owners have done a great job restoring it."

"We'll have to do that," Carl said. "Frank, have you got a minute to help me find some water for Hero? I'd like to be sure he's hydrated before we go traipsing about in that heat."

"Of course!" Frank replied, pushing his wheelchair back. "How shall we do this?"

"I'll hold on to a handle of your chair in one hand and keep Hero's harness in the other. Wheel away, my friend."

"You got it!"

It only took a few minutes to find a water fountain, where Carl filled a collapsible water dish he'd pulled from his backpack. While Hero lapped the cool liquid eagerly, Carl turned to Frank.

"What are you doing, Frank?" he asked.

"What?" Frank asked, not sure what Carl was referring to.

"You and Janet. What are you doing?"

"What about Janet and me?" Frank frowned.

"Are you really just friends, or are you just afraid to make it official?"

Frank thought furiously. He was decidedly uncomfortable at this line of questioning. He decided to play dumb.

"Official?"

Carl chuckled. "Oh, no. You're not getting off that easily. I may be blind, but I can hear the love in her voice when she talks to you. I can hear the same in yours when you mention her name. You two are meant for each other."

"We're just…"

"No," Carl interrupted. "Whatever you choose to call it, you're more than friends." He leaned down and fumbled to find Frank's shoulder. Placing his hand there, he seemed to be looking directly into Frank's soul. "Don't put it off, Frank. You have a wonderful woman who would jump at the chance to be part of your life permanently. Don't let her get away. Don't wait for something to pull you apart. Make it official. Today, if possible."

With that, Carl straightened, then bent down to retrieve the now empty water dish. Shaking the last drops out, he collapsed it and put it back into his backpack.

"Now, I think it's time Mel and I checked out those old cars he's so fond of! Lead me back, my friend."

Without a word, Frank waited just a moment for Carl to place his hand on the wheelchair, then he wheeled back to the table where Janet and Mel were chuckling together.

"What's so funny?" he asked.

"Just a childhood memory," Mel replied. "Janet can share it with you later. I want to see the cars before my joints get any older!"

With a laugh and a round of handshakes, the brothers wandered off.

"Did you want to look at more cars, or are you ready to call it a day?" Janet asked.

Frank didn't answer for a moment. When he did, he reached over and took Janet's hand.

"Actually, I am tired and ready to go home, but there's something I want to ask you first."

Epilogue

Janet waited anxiously at the transit center for Frank's bus to arrive. For some reason, she'd been nervous ever since the car show when Frank had invited her on what he called an "official date". She and Frank had been doing things together as friends for a couple of months now, but calling this an official date seemed to change her comfort level.

She'd become quite accustomed to meeting Frank for coffee, or going to a movie together, or hanging out in the park and watching the children play. She didn't mind pushing his chair when the terrain was rough or walking beside him when he insisted on pushing himself. She enjoyed his witty banter and loved his broad smile. She admired his courage and tenacity, his huge heart and giving nature. His ice-blue eyes never failed to mesmerize her. His laugh always made her heart sing.

So, why was she nervous now? Did a label change anything?

No, she told herself firmly. He's the same Frank, and I'm the same Janet. We're just having dinner like we do every Saturday.

Hm. Like every Saturday. Her brows furrowed as she considered that realization. When had her feelings for him changed from friendship to…

Her thoughts were interrupted by the arrival of the route nine bus. She took a step forward and watched the passengers step out the back door. Turning her attention to the front, she watched as the lift began its creaky journey from the darkened interior into the bright sunlight.

Suddenly, her jaw dropped. She expected to see Frank wheel off the lift in his chair. She did not expect to see him standing behind a walker. He looked up, spotted her, and grinned a boyish are-you-proud-of-me grin.

When the achingly slow lift finally rested on the concrete sidewalk, he looked back down and pushed the walker forward, stepping carefully behind it.

Janet was frozen in place. Tears filled her eyes as she watched Frank carefully close the distance between them. When he reached her, he looked up again, his grin growing even broader.

"Surprised?" he asked.

Taking a deep breath, Janet tried to regain control of her emotions. "Am I ever! What's this?" She gestured toward the walker.

"It's a walker," Frank said with a chuckle.

"I know it's a walker," Janet replied, slapping his arm in mock frustration. "When did you start using it? How…"

"It's a long story, and I'm starving," he responded. "Can I tell you over dinner?"

"Sure. Where did you want to eat?"

They picked a restaurant close to the transit center. Janet marveled with each step Frank took, but she noticed he looked pretty tired by the time they'd walked the block and a half to the restaurant.

Once they were seated, he took a deep breath and let it out slowly. "Amazing! I didn't think I'd ever be able to do that again!"

"Walk?" she asked.

"Nope, take my best girl to dinner!" he quipped.

Janet's eyebrows shot up. "Your best girl?"

"Yup. My best girl," he repeated, his voice softening as he reached for her hand. "Will you be my best girl, Janet?"

Unbidden, tears filled her eyes as she smiled. "I'd be honored, Frank."

Janet didn't know what other surprises life held for her, but this, she was sure, would always be at the top of her "best moments ever" list.

The End…

Or is it the beginning of something even more wonderful?

Coming Soon

Conscious Compassion

Lifting the World, Book 2

FERRELL HORNSBY

Summer 2020

About the Author

Ferrell Hornsby has been writing stories and poetry since she could hold a pencil in her chubby, little hand. Encouraged by her grandmother, she continued writing, even after receiving her first rejection letter at age twelve.

Since then, she explored many genres but found new passion (pun intended) when she discovered historical romance! She thrilled to the combination of historical settings, suspenseful adventures, and new love blossoming.

After publishing three historical fiction novels under the pseudonym Emily Daniels, she decided to branch out to another genre, inspirational fiction, choosing this time to use her real name.

Pulling from her own life experiences, and those of her husband, her stories now have a depth and emotional component that will have the reader laughing and crying in turn. (Keep the tissues handy, folks!)

Ferrell married her soul mate in 2011, and together, they enjoy music, movies, travel, and ice cream (the more chocolate, the better).

If you'd like more information or inspiration about the Lifting the World movement, you can find us at:

https://www.facebook.com/groups/Lifting TheWorld/

Also, at:

https://lift-the-world.com/